Pulphouse

FICTION MAGAZINE

Issue Thirty-Two

Magazine Editor
Dean Wesley Smith

A WMG Publishing Magazine

Pulphouse Fiction Magazine Issue #32
Published by WMG Publishing Inc.
Cover and interior design copyright © 2024 WMG Publishing Inc.
Cover art copyright © grandfailure/Depositphotos
Small creature we call Thumper copyright © beutoszig/Depositphotos

Pulphouse
FICTION MAGAZINE

TABLE OF CONTENTS

Pulphouse Fiction Magazine
A WMG Publishing Magazine

Editor
Dean Wesley Smith

Executive Editor
Kristine Kathryn Rusch

Director of Operations
Stephanie Writt

FROM THE EDITOR'S DESK
SUMMER IN THE CITY

The summer here in Las Vegas is like the dead of winter in northern states and regions around the world. For three months, we just don't go out in the weather without being prepared and having a plan.

Our problem here is not the deep cold of three months of

winter, but extreme heat of June, July, and August. Sometimes deadly heat.

One hundred and ten and 5% humidity is common. (You can't feel yourself sweat because it dries instantly.)

The rest of the year, Las Vegas is a wonderful town for the weather. Sun seems to always be shining, we can walk anywhere, and sure, there are a few storms just to keep things from being boring, but they blow over quickly and fill the lakes with much-needed water.

For the summer, Kris and I are luckier than many who live here. We have indoor parking for our cars, so we get into a cool car and often drive to another parking garage. For many trips we never even feel the heat.

Grocery store walks from the car to the store and back to a hot car are the most common time in those three months that I even notice the heat. Or from the car to the gym. Yeah, I know, tough life.

But no time in those three months am I in the heat longer than a few minutes. I have suffered my share of heat strokes over my lifetime and they are no laughing matter.

But like the three winter months of other parts of the world, the extreme weather here forces you to do the inside things you have wanted to do. For me, that is writing and reading.

Amazing how important those two things become when they are taken away from you as reading was for me for months when I went blind with an eye infection, and writing when I broke my shoulder and could not type for four months.

So honestly, I am enjoying the heat this summer. I am sure

I will be ready for it to move out when September gets here so I can get back to walking places and being in 5K races, but for now I can enjoy the somewhat forced time indoors.

And all the reading and writing I get to do.

I sure hope you enjoy reading the stories in this issue. There are some great ones.

DEAN WESLEY SMITH
LAS VEGAS, NEVADA

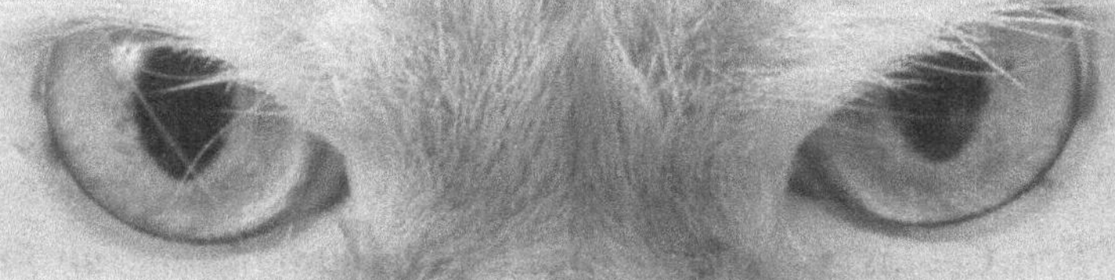

BRIGID COLLINS

Professional writer Brigid Collins is the daughter of professional writer Ron Collins. Clearly the incredible writing skills run in the family. She has sold many stories over the years, including some to Pulphouse Collections *and to* Fiction River. *And as a team with her father, she sometimes is a guest editor for* Fiction River.

In fact, she and her dad will be once again editing a Fiction River *volume in the restart of the* Fiction River *series. Watch for that in 2025.*

In this wonderfully original story, Brigid gives us a character with a great voice and attitude that you won't soon forget.

PART OF A BALANCED BREAKFAST

BRIGID COLLINS

Derrick knew that, as the new guy on the night shift at Papa Gerry's 24-hour Green Grocer, he was due for a little hazing. In fact, he was kind of looking forward to it.

A guy like him didn't often get to experience such rites of passage, given he was a bit too muscle-bulked from all his years of high school weight training and wrestling. But now he was in the summer months ahead of his freshman year at good old State College, officially majoring in Undecided, and while he wasn't really interested in joining a fraternity, he did have the common need that plagued all college students: money. Thus, a part-time job at the local grocery, where his employee discount would allow him to stretch each hour's seven dollars and fifty cents into a few extra packs of ramen and maybe even some fresh produce once in a while.

And his coworkers who didn't know him yet could haze him just as well, if not better, than any frat brother, even if they were all a lot of skinny goth kids who looked like they'd be better suited to writing terrible poetry than hauling crates of milk out to restock.

So when the shift leader came over to him as he clocked in for his ten PM shift, a glint of superiority in her heavily lined eye, Derrick drew his shoulders in so he looked less hulky than usual and put a resigned smile on his face.

It helped that the shift leader was kinda cute, for a goth.

"You've got aisle seven tonight," she said, snappy. Her black hair swayed in twin ponytails as she walked, the pink fringe of her bangs cutting just above her eye makeup. The big friendly Papa Gerry's nametag pinned to her vest had "Vanessa" scrawled on it in sharp black letters.

Behind her, the rest of the coven sat on the pile of unopened boxes of pickle jars and ketchup bottles and sniggered like they were pulling a fast one on Derrick.

Derrick shrugged. "No prob. What's wrong with it?"

"Wrong?" Shift Leader Vanessa lifted one dark eyebrow. "Nothing. It's cereal and granola bars. Big guy like you seems like he should be able to handle a bit of breakfast."

More sniggering.

"Sure," Derrick agreed. "But I'm the new guy, so there's got to be something bad about this assignment. Honestly, kinda surprised I'm not on bathroom duty."

"No way," said one of the coven. His voice was higher than Derrick would have expected, and his eyes were rimmed with red in a way that looked more like he'd been smoking something than crying artfully over his latest word sculpture. "Those toilets are mine. Porcelain's an insulator. I'll keep my dulcet aromas of shit, and the rest of you fucks can deal with the ghost."

"Oh," said Derrick. "Aisle seven's haunted?" That was fun. He could play along. He used to play Frankenstein monsters in the Halloween corn mazes back home.

Shift Leader Vanessa rolled her eyes. They were blue, he noticed. And so unimpressed by his good-natured farm boy thing. "Only a little bit. Don't worry about it. Just get those oat bars restocked before midnight and we won't have a problem, yeah?"

Derrick nodded, loaded his handcart with a palette of prepackaged breakfast bars and sugary cereals, and hulked his way down to the definitely haunted aisle seven.

He was ready for anything. Boxes knocked off the shelf behind his back, spooky moaning coming from aisles six and eight, even bedsheets flapped around the endcaps to complete the prank.

Maybe if he could act like he was really scared, then laugh and admit that they totally got him when the prank was revealed, Shift Leader Vanessa might not sneer at him when he worked up the guts to ask her on a date.

The wheels of his handcart squeaked when he stopped at the end of aisle seven. He paused there, making a show of looking a little nervous. There was a bit of a chill to the air, actually. The whole store was over-airconditioned to hell, of course, but there must be a draft or an air vent right overhead here that had Derrick giving a genuine shiver.

The aisle was empty of customers, but so were most of the aisles at ten o'clock at night.

Carefully, he maneuvered the cart and palette to the

middle of the aisle and squatted down to start unpacking the goods.

He worked for a few minutes, shuffling boxes so the expiration dates were soonest up front. FIFO, he'd been told by the training video yesterday, was more than an acronym. It was a way of life.

A loud *clap* to his right made him jump.

When he looked, a box of cereal had fallen to the middle of the floor, face-down so the cartoonish kids' activities on the back asked the ceiling if it could find three differences or trace its way to the bowl of processed wheat at the center of the maze.

Stifling a chuckle, Derrick made himself gasp in fear. Then he strained his ears for the hiss of goth laughter the next aisle over.

It didn't come. Maybe he was overdoing his bit. He lowered his hand from where he'd pressed it against his chest, then went to pick the box up. With a satisfied nod, he put it back where it had fallen from. Then, he picked it back up, and pulled the box behind it up front. The expiration date on that one was sooner than on the one that had fallen.

Done, he turned back to his palette.

A woman stood between him and it.

He jumped again, startled for real. He might have let out a little shriek, even.

The woman tipped her head to one side, looking even less impressed with him than Shift Leader Vanessa had. She had the handles of a plastic Papa Gerry's grocery basket looped over one arm. "Excuse me," she said in a prim tone.

"Sorry, ma'am," Derrick said, trying to make his heartbeat return to normal. "You just startled me. Can I help you?"

"I certainly hope so. I'm looking for… *Frosty Pops*," she said. She leaned forward a bit as she named the product, and her eyes widened slightly. "They're part of a balanced breakfast."

Derrick fought the urge to lean back. "Um. I… don't think I've heard of those…"

"They're part of a balanced breakfast," the woman repeated as if he hadn't heard her.

Now Derrick was fighting the urge to laugh. Of course. The goths had pulled a customer into their hazing. The woman obviously wasn't a ghost. Flesh and blood held that basket up, and Derrick couldn't see through her even a little bit.

They'd done a good job of theming, though. The groceries she had in her basket were all breakfasty things: eggs, milk, a pack of bacon, a single large grapefruit, and a bottle of orange juice. Balanced, indeed.

"I'm very sorry, ma'am," he said, putting on his best country-boy smile. "Let me just call to see if we've got any— Frosty Pops, was it?— in the back."

He turned to head for the pole at the end of the aisle, where the phone that would let him speak over the store-wide intercom hung. He wasn't embarrassed to let his voice crackle out over the mostly empty store asking for an item check on something he was pretty sure didn't exist.

The hand that dropped onto his shoulder was both heavy enough to make him stagger and cold enough to raise his entire skin to goosebumps.

Derrick twisted to look over his shoulder, then wished he hadn't.

The woman's hair was floating around her head like a wreath of snakes, and her face was going hollow and skeletal before his eyes. Her prim, white dress flapped exactly like those bedsheets he'd envisioned, except he *could* see through them now, and through her arms and legs. The basket she'd held crashed to the floor. Milk and OJ sprayed over the shelves in a nauseating mixture. Eggs splattered on the linoleum. The grapefruit bounced along the aisle, picking up an entire battery of bruises.

"Frosty Pops! They're part of a balanced breakfast!" the woman screamed.

"Holy shit," Derrick said, shaking where she held him.

Then, something truly horrific happened.

The woman pulled away, her expression pinching into the look all customer service workers feared most.

Derrick took his newfound freedom and stumbled backwards, his lungs squeezing against a scream that tried to claw its way out of his throat. But no matter how quick he moved, he couldn't get out of aisle seven before she spoke the dreaded words.

"I want to speak to your managerrrrr!"

Derrick made it to the pole with the phone amidst a wailing wind of ghostly screams and malevolence.

"C-Customer Service to a-a-aisle seven!" he yelled into the receiver. "And, uh, maybe an exorcist!"

———

"Wow," said the toilet-loving goth in breathless reverence. "He got her to ask for his manager on his first encounter."

His name was Jace, according to his nametag. The piercing in his left eyebrow sparkled in the harsh fluorescent light of the employee breakroom, where Derrick was recuperating from said *encounter*.

"Jesus," Derrick said, hunching further around the bag of Cheetos Vanessa had gotten for him by kicking the rattly vending machine in the corner. "I thought you guys were just hazing me."

"Nah. Aisle seven's totally haunted," Vanessa said. "Mama's been there trying to bring her *balanced breakfast* to the little ghost toddlers back home for years, apparently. Longer than I've worked here. But we do make newbies check her out ASAP. Night shift's gotta know we've got capable workers, you know."

Derrick glanced up at her, uncertain which of the thousand questions he ought to ask.

Vanessa met his look, then, after a moment, pursed her

lips to the side and admitted, "You did good. She likes it when Customer Service comes to her. Eat your Cheetos."

Obediently, Derrick lifted a cheese puff to his mouth. The flavor was sharp enough to cut through his shock, at least. He ate another one.

"Hasn't anyone ever tried to… y'know…" he said.

"Calm her restless spirit?" Vanessa asked. "Yeah. Thing is, all she wants are her damned Frosty Pops, and those were discontinued in the nineties."

Jace let out a high laugh. "Get this. The factory where they made 'em? Burned down. The recipe? Inside the factory. Those Frosty Pops are gone the way of all the good shit anyone halfway remembers from the rosy days of childhood."

"Mama's gonna be trying to balance her breakfast until the heat death of the universe," Vanessa said. "Us friendly members of Papa Gerry's family have just decided to work around her."

"That's kind of sad," Derrick said. His Cheetos bag crinkled in his fingers.

"Most ghost stories are, Muscles," Vanessa said with a shrug. "So. Wanna keep working here? Or would you rather split?"

She cast her dark-lined eyes over him, daring him to meet her challenge, expecting him to disappoint her.

Derrick took a deep breath, then let it out. "Muscles?"

Shift Leader Vanessa's black-painted lips quirked up, just a little. "Unless you wanna fight the Porcelain Prince here for *his* title."

"Hey!"

Despite his lingering shivers, Derrick grinned. "You don't get muscles like mine or pristine porcelain kingdoms like his without doing hard work and overcoming a few obstacles." He met Vanessa's blue eyes and nodded.

"I'm in."

THE NIGHT SHIFT was pretty uneventful, most of the time.

It turned out the coven of goths didn't actually work there, just Shift Leader Vanessa and Porcelain Prince Jace and Double Hex Katy, the quiet high school dropout who wore safety pins in her ear piercings and worked Customer Service. The rest liked to hang out in the back sometimes because it was a good place to smoke when the weather was too pleasant for their dismal demeanors, or too rainy.

Derrick kind of thought he ought to get a two-word nickname, too, but when he voiced the thought Shift Leader Vanessa simply lifted one thickly-penciled eyebrow and stared at him pointedly, until he said "yeah, okay," and went to hulk another palette of dried pasta to aisle five.

They did get customers from time to time. Mostly drunk students looking for cheap munchies or just a way to kill some boredom in the last few weeks before classes started up again, but sometimes they got a frazzled soccer mom grabbing a last-minute rotisserie chicken for a super-late family dinner, or a slick businessman still yammering into his hands-free cell phone like a maniac as he rang himself through the self-checkout line for a bunch of bananas, a box of snack cakes, and a bottle of lotion.

Derrick learned not to judge people's carts. Much.

Mostly, he pointed people to the correct aisle to find what they were looking for, and he restocked shelves.

He did see Mama a few times a week. Each time he had to restock aisle seven, she was there. She didn't always approach him, though. Sometimes, she just stared forlornly at the shelves as if her Frosty Pops might materialize if she just looked long enough.

The times she did approach him were not as dramatic as that first time. Maybe that was just because he knew what to expect now, or maybe it was because she was in a calmer mood. Derrick didn't know. He just did his best to be kind and accommodating when she did ask him. His sweet country-boy smile got a ton of use with her. He had to call Double Hex Katy to come soothe her only twice in his first two weeks of work.

"Does she ever show up during the day shift?" he asked as he and Katy were clocking out after that second call.

She shrugged as she grabbed her card from the slot on the

wall. "Papa Gerry's doesn't appear on the lists of haunted locations around campus."

Derrick waited, but she didn't elaborate. She punched her card, swung her black Hello Kitty purse over her shoulder, and twitched her fingers in a goodbye sigil.

Derrick punched his own card in mild exasperation. Of course there were lists of haunted locations, and of course Double Hex Katy had them all memorized. But, he supposed, if the grocery store wasn't on any of them, that meant Mama's existence wasn't common knowledge. He couldn't remember ever seeing any nighttime customers go down aisle seven, as if perhaps the place gave off a "do not disturb" vibe. Maybe only those on the night shift even knew about Mama at all.

Were they trying to keep it that way? Shift Leader Vanessa hadn't sat him down and made him swear any blood promises or recite a metered oath of secrecy when he agreed to keep working here. She also hadn't implied that they had ways of making him keep what he knew quiet — or, for that matter, making him not know it any more. But there was Katy's nick-name, the origin of which he had no freaking clue about.

Still, when he thought on it, something about the idea of exposing Mama and her plight to the general public sat wrong with him. You didn't make Grammy Claire and her forgetfulness into a side show at the state fair, or let strangers gawk at your kid sister's attempts to speak past her stutter.

You also didn't sit back and make them struggle through on their own. Even if there wasn't anything you could do to fix the problem, you still let them know you were right there with them the whole time.

Derrick looked down at the punch card still in his hand.

He had a neat row of times in and out now, two whole weeks' worth of ten-to-six shifts. In another pair of weeks, he'd have to consider changing his shift to accommodate the 7:00 AM English 101 class he'd had to sign up for. He'd never expected to feel an emotional connection to a work shift at a kitschy grocery store, and yet here he was, having a pang in his heart at the thought of leaving.

Maybe Double Hex Katy had already worked some magic over him while he wasn't looking.

Shaking his head, he put the punch card back in its slot on the wall and walked out into the lightening morning.

———

"Hey, man. Can you tell me where the ginger ale is?"

Derrick looked up from the endcap where he was affixing sale tags on Oreos and smiled at the clearly drunk guy swaying beside him. The guy's sweater displayed the good old State College name under a judicious and aromatic beer stain.

"Sodas are in aisle four," Derrick said.

"Yeah. Definitely. I looked there, man, but I didn't see the kind I want."

"Oh, I'm sorry. What kind were you looking for? We might not stock it, but I can—"

"Excuse me."

The prim voice cut through Derrick's polite explanations like a cold knife, and he froze on the spot. He wasn't standing in aisle seven. The endcap he'd been working was between seven and six. He hadn't been prepared to see her.

Carefully, he glanced to his left. Sure enough, there she

was, white dress perfectly pressed and Papa Gerry's basket full of a nearly balanced breakfast hanging from her arm. She was standing with the toes of her white pumps right on the edge of the last linoleum tile of aisle seven. Her torso was slightly leaned forward over that invisible barrier he'd never seen her cross before.

"Do you have any Frosty Pops?"

"Dude," said the drunk guy. "My ginger ale?"

Derrick's breath came suddenly quick and shallow, and he whipped back around to his living customer. Had the guy noticed Mama? Did he even see her? He was obviously too flushed to notice the chill in the air, and even if he did, the refrigerated dairy section behind them could more easily explain it. Derrick didn't know if anything bad would happen if a customer saw her, but he didn't want it to happen, and definitely not on his watch.

He took a careful step to put his bulk between Mama and the guy. Which did mean putting his back to Mama, but he'd done that before while stocking her aisle.

Of course, she hadn't been asking him to help her find her Frosty Pops those times.

"Uh, right. Um. What kind were you looking for?" he asked in what he hoped was a bright and friendly tone.

Drunk Guy blinked and tilted his head to look over Derrick's shoulder, confusion bubbling up from under the sheen of inebriation. "I don't remember what it's called, actually."

"Frosty Pops are part of a *balanced* breakfast."

Derrick jumped.

Mama was leaning all the way around him. Her feet were

still firmly planted in aisle seven, so her body was stretched almost to the point of unnatural to achieve this. Her eyes were narrowed in disdain as she looked Drunk Guy up and down as if summing up every poor decision the guy had ever made in one fell swoop. He would be a bad influence on her ghost toddlers, that was for sure.

Interesting that she'd never looked that way at Vanessa or Katy, or even Jace, despite their piercings and black hair dye and Jace's ever-present haze of weed. Derrick was pretty sure he'd seen the edge of a tattoo under the hem of Vanessa's shirt, too, when she'd stretched to reach a bottle of Sriracha sauce down from the top shelf for someone the other day. Not that he'd been *looking*. He'd just seen it, that was all. And thought about it all the next day.

None of which was important right now as Mama and the Drunk Guy stared each other down around all Derrick's ineffectual hulk.

"I guess so, lady. But I don't need breakfast. Ginger ale settles my stomach."

And, as if on purpose, Drunk Guy belched.

Derrick, having spent many hours in the locker rooms after already having had his nose pressed into the wrestling mat by another guy's hairy, sweaty armpit, was no stranger to manly stenches. That didn't mean he wasn't offended, or disgusted. He reeled backwards, hand flying to cover his nose as the sour odor wafted directly at him.

His shoulder blade bumped into Mama, and she, still solid enough to hold her basket, stumbled.

The moment her foot touched the floor beyond aisle seven, the lights in the whole store began flickering.

"Whoa," said Drunk Guy, swaying and raising a hand to his head. "Whoa, that's trippy."

"Ah?" said Mama. It was a sound caught somewhere between bewildered and scared.

Derrick's hands were automatically reaching to steady her as he would anyone else he'd bumped his mass into. He didn't think, he simply took hold of her arms and, firmly but gently, picked her up and set her back within the bounds of aisle seven.

His heart was pounding so hard he could feel it throbbing in his toes.

The lights had stopped flickering, though.

"Mama, why don't you wait right here, and I'll go look for your Frosty Pops just as soon as I'm done helping this person. Okay?"

Mama blinked up at him, her mouth open just a smidge more than a living person could manage, her eyes burning with frustrated confusion. "They're… they're the best way for a kid to start the morning."

"I know, Mama," Derrick said, nodding. "That's why you'll wait here? For me to come back?"

"I *am* looking for Frosty Pops," she said. She was looking more sure of herself again, her voice sounding more like her usual prim self. She stood straighter and readjusted the Papa Gerry's basket on her arm.

"Hey man, does your mom need, like, *help* or something?"

Derrick wrestled his best country-boy smile to his face before whirling on Drunk Guy. "She's fine. Let's go see about your ginger ale."

But he wasn't certain Mama was fine. As he marched Drunk Guy back to aisle four, he couldn't help glancing back.

Mama stood at the edge of aisle seven again, leaning over it to watch him leave.

Overhead, the lights gave one faint flicker.

When he finally convinced Drunk Guy to take the off-brand soda and scurried back to aisle seven, Mama was gone.

A WEEK and a half before the fall semester started, Jace tackled Derrick in front of the deli counter. His eyes were wide and bright, and the usual red rim was faded. He was shivering so hard his eyebrow piercing glinted like a strobe light.

"Dude. *Dude!* She's *in the men's room*. She's standing between the urinals and screaming at the soap dispenser about her *goddamned Frosty Pops!*"

Derrick transferred the heavy ham to one hand and put the other on Jace's shoulder. The guy was spooked for sure. He was breathing so fast he'd blown away most of the clinging aura of weed. "Hey, take a deep breath. It's okay. I thought you said porcelain was an insulator?"

"Oh, come on. I was just making shit up. But what is she doing in my bathrooms? That was my *safe haven*."

"Maybe she needs to take a whizz?" Derrick tried.

Jace glared at him so hard Derrick felt the angry poetry scrawling itself around his head.

Derrick held one hand up. "Okay, okay. Let's go take a look."

Sure enough, Mama was in the men's room. She was no

longer standing between the urinals, but now was addressing the hand dryer, which was blowing at full power and making her white dress flutter against her legs. Her basket was sitting on the floor, a sight that made Derrick wince instantly, while she scolded the machine.

"*Part* of a balanced breakfast!" she shouted over the noise. "*Part* of it!"

Derrick leaned towards Jace where he'd frozen in the doorway. "Did you try calling Double Hex Katy?" he muttered.

Jace gave a tight shake of his head, never taking his eyes off Mama. "Not in tonight."

Oh. That was right. Katy had the night off, which meant there was no Customer Service to call if things went bad.

All right. Things simply wouldn't go bad, then.

Derrick rolled his shoulders and stepped fully into the men's room. Jace had left his mop bucket full of solution right inside the door, the mop handle leaning like a parking garage gate across the entryway. Derrick lifted the mop and passed under it, then set it back down gently. The harsh scent of cleaning agents stung his eyes, but he smiled through it.

"Hey, Mama," he said loudly to be heard over the roaring hand dryer. "Can I help you find something?"

Mama whirled on him. Her eyes were as wide and wild as Jace's, her hair floating in a way that couldn't be explained by the blower.

Derrick didn't falter, though he had to swallow against the squeeze of fear in his throat. "Cereal is aisle seven. Why don't we go back there and see if we can't find your Frosty Pops?"

Mama took a step towards him, and the lights over the

mirror buzzed. She took another, and the hand dryer abruptly cut off.

"They're not there," she whispered into the ringing silence. "Don't lie to me."

Behind Derrick, Jace freaked out.

"Shit. Shit. Shitshit*shit*fuck."

That was poetry Derrick could understand. What he couldn't understand was the sound of the men's room door slamming shut behind him as Jace abandoned ship.

So much for coworker camaraderie. If Papa Gerry's ever held a team-building outing, Derrick was totally letting Jace hit the ground during his trust fall.

Mama took another step towards him. Her fists were clenched in her skirt, and her face was getting that hollow, death's head look she'd gotten his first night on the job. One of the toilets flushed on its own.

Derrick lifted his hands, palms out. His fingers were shaking. He didn't think he'd be able to bodily lift her like he'd done a few days ago, even if doing so would have accomplished anything. She probably wouldn't appreciate a hug at this point.

"I'm sorry, Mama. You're right. The truth is, we don't carry Frosty Pops."

As if his words were a pin, Mama deflated like a balloon. She slumped backwards, not quite falling to her knees, arms dangling so her fingertips almost brushed her heels, and her head tipping up to stare at the ceiling tiles, her jaw slack. She let out a long sound of anguish that Derrick felt in the depths of his chest.

"All the vitamins and nutrients a growing kid neeeeeds," she moaned.

Some of Derrick's fear loosened, and he took the final step to close the distance between them. Maybe she *would* like a hug.

"Have you tried Cheerios?" he asked.

Mama's slack jaw closed with a loud snap. She turned her head to stare at him, and a wave of freezing air crashed over him so suddenly he gasped.

Her hands were on him, squeezing his biceps like she meant to dig her bony fingers into his meat. Her face loomed over his. Fury radiated from her eyes and her grimacing lips.

Derrick was on his knees, and he didn't even care that his jeans were pressed against the filthy, unmopped men's room floor. Mama was above him, pressing and pressing.

Escape it, his years of training commanded. *Granby roll and knee pick her to the mat!*

But he couldn't move. Against Mama's hold, he was helpless.

She leaned closer, mouth opening.

The door burst open. Vanessa strode in, sending the leaning mop clattering to the floor in a splash of cleaning solution. Her twin black ponytails swayed behind her. Her Papa Gerry's vest blazed emerald in the fluorescent light. She looked beautiful as hell.

"Ma'am, if you can't respect the employees here, I'm gonna have to ask you to leave."

She said it strong and forceful, as if her authority as shift leader really did give her the jurisdiction to banish Mama from the store.

Derrick couldn't tell if he was holding his breath more out of terror or awe.

A moment passed as Vanessa stared Mama down.

Then, Mama flinched. Her hands lifted from Derrick's arms, and when he let out a sigh of relief, she recoiled with a hiss. Like a jealous cave creature, she scuttled back to her basket and picked it up, clutching it to her chest. Then, casting one last burning glare at Derrick, she vanished.

He should feel relieved. Instead, he felt like the worst kind of slime.

"You all right, Muscles?"

Carefully, Derrick got to his feet. Numbness tingled through his whole body. "I'll live," he said.

Vanessa looked him up and down, then nodded. "Go take a break. I'll clean up in here."

Grateful and ashamed, Derrick left.

<hr>

THE REST of the shift went by without a single customer, which was good, since there was no sign of Jace anywhere. Derrick and Vanessa tag-teamed manning the front and taking care of the cleaning and restocking. Neither of them saw Mama again, but a pervasive chill lingered in the air no matter where Derrick worked, so he knew she was still there, somewhere.

When it finally came time to clock out, his shoulders were so tense he could barely lift his arms.

Outside, the sky was beginning to pink up, and a fog was

rising from the asphalt of the back alley. It was still pretty dark, though.

A dim ember blazed in the shadowed nook across from the dumpster as Derrick passed.

Jace was leaning against the brick wall, shoulders hunched in the black raincoat he wore no matter the weather. The fringe of his hair dangled limply over his eyebrow piercing.

"Hey," Derrick said.

"Hey." Jace lifted his sloppily-rolled joint to his lips and took a long drag. Then he let the smoke out in a thin wisp. "Sorry."

"It's okay."

"It's fucking not. She just… reminds me of someone."

Derrick hesitated, then said, "Your mother?"

"No, not my fucking *mom*, dickhead."

Derrick felt himself smile. Hefting his bag higher on his shoulder, he stepped over to join Jace in leaning against the wall. When Jace held the joint out, he took it. The rancid-sweet flavor curled in his mouth as he took a pull, but when he breathed out his shoulders finally unknotted.

"My brother," Jace said as he took the joint back. "He used to take care of me. Make sure I had enough to eat. Shit like that."

"Sounds like a good guy. What happened?"

Jace shrugged. "Dad hit him enough times to make him leave. Then he hit me enough times to make me leave. But I always wondered why Robbie didn't take me with him. Like, I dunno. It's fine. I can take care of myself now. But he put all that effort into stuffing good food into me and shit, and then he just… gave up. Decided I wasn't worth it anymore, I guess.

I dunno." He lifted the joint to his lips again, then exhaled more smoke. "Then here's Mama, dead as fuck, and she's still trying to get her kids a decent breakfast. I mean, I don't know her story, but it still makes me angry."

Derrick winced. "Hell."

"Yeah."

They passed the joint between them a couple more times. The sky grew pinker, then turned gray. The fog around them thinned as it burned off.

The back door of Papa Gerry's squealed open, and Vanessa came out into the morning. She looked tired, her pink bangs sweat-straggled, her black-lined eyes hooded and bagged. But Derrick's heart still gave a twinge when her blue eyes locked onto his. He remembered the cool authority of her standing in the men's room doorway and commanding Mama to leave him alone.

Then she glanced at the stubby end of the joint with a sigh. "Spare a hit?"

Jace held it out. The glowing ember cast a sprinkle of orange light over her face as she plucked it from his fingers and took a drag. As she blew the smoke out, she dropped the stub to the asphalt and ground her heel over it.

"See you boys tomorrow," she said, then walked the rest of the way through the alley to the street where her car was parked. The rumble of her motor sounded a moment later.

Derrick glanced at Jace to find Jace glancing at him. He almost laughed.

"I'll be here," he said. He felt suddenly fortified, his muscles all loose from the weed. Tonight had been terrifying, but that feeling Mama had left him with was still there, unresolved.

He wasn't tapping out yet.

Jace nodded, then pushed away from the wall. He slumped off down the alleyway, too, hands in his raincoat pockets and shoulders hunched as if in dejection. But there was a certain strength to his stride that told Derrick he'd see the goth poet right on time for tomorrow's shift.

Derrick watched him leave, lost in thought for a long moment. Then he resettled his bag on his shoulder and headed off towards his dorm.

It had been a long time since he'd wondered what it would have been like to have a brother.

THAT MORNING, before sliding into bed, Derrick did what he should have done ages ago.

He Googled Frosty Pops.

"I'M SORRY," Double Hex Katy said, shaking her head and blinking rapidly. Her black Hello Kitty purse dangled like a pendulum from her hand, which was paused halfway to stowing it in her locker before their shift. "You've had an idea for *what* now?"

"A seance," Derrick said. "I thought that was the sort of thing you, you know, did." He wiggled his fingers, miming casting a spell.

Double Hex Katy glowered at him. Though she was two

years younger than him, that glower made her seem so much more worldly.

"A seance," she repeated, deadpan. "For *cereal?*"

"Why not? It's as dead as any ghost. Discontinued, factory burned, recipe lost. Why can't we call up its spirit and get Mama to, like, commune with it or whatever?"

The look she levered on him told him he was an absolute idiot. But he could handle being an idiot if it meant trying something. When he didn't back down, she sighed, stuffed her purse into her locker, and slammed the door. "Did you run this by Shift Leader Vanessa yet?"

Derrick smiled. "So you *can* do it?"

Katy scoffed. "Muscles, *nobody* can call up the spirit of something that doesn't have one. It's not dead, because it wasn't ever alive to begin with."

"Well, technically, there's the wheat that got processed, and the corn for the high fructose corn syrup, and the sugar cane they used for the frosting, and some people think there was even some rice in the recipe, and—"

"Alright, alright, shut *up.* Lilith save me from your masculine urges to *well-actually.* Again, did you talk to Vanessa? And what about Jace?"

"Don't worry about Jace. He's solid. Vanessa's cool with it if you think you can do it. I told her you had it."

A strange thing happened to Double Hex Katy's face. It turned, ever so faintly, pink.

"Huh. You did. Well. I mean, I guess it would definitely be fun to try. There's some stuff I could— Although maybe— Look, I'll get back to you, okay? I've got some ideas. Hmm… wheat germ and a white-sage-and-rosemary smudge…"

She wandered toward the Customer Service counter, muttering to herself as she shouldered her Papa Gerry's vest on.

Derrick watched her for a moment, satisfied. Then he grabbed his trusty handcart and went to restock the tomato sauce.

———————

THREE DAYS before the fall semester at good old State College began, they held their seance.

It was midnight, of course. And while they couldn't actually close the store, Double Hex Katy prepared the space by spilling a line of salt across the entryway and drawing a sigil in the air with a burning stick of incense. The scent of cinnamon and sandalwood lingered even after she stubbed the fire out.

Now they sat in a circle — a square? a diamond? — on the floor in the exact middle of aisle seven, holding hands around a white pillar candle, a small carved wooden bowl, and three little piles of powder: flour, corn starch, and sugar. Derrick sat across from Katy, with Vanessa on his left and Jace on his right.

Anticipation thrummed through every one of Derrick's muscles. It was like being on the edge of the mat right before facing the best guy from a rival school.

Katy leaned forward and lit the candle. Then, with her finger, she drew a circle through the three piles, pulling wheat into corn, corn into sugar, sugar into wheat.

"And thus the cycle continues," she said as she took Vanessa's hand again. "We call upon the gestalt spirits that linger here, greater together than the sum of their parts. We call upon… *Frosty Pops*."

Together, as they'd practiced, Derrick, Vanessa, and Jace chanted, "They're part of a balanced breakfast."

For a moment, nothing happened. Then, Derrick noticed he couldn't hear the hum of the dairy section's refrigerators. When he looked at the center of their circle, he thought he saw a faint stirring in the three powders.

But… that was all. For a long, awkward silence, the powders moved a little. Then they stopped. Slowly, the refrigerators rattled back to life.

"Damn," Jace said. "I guess it's not gonna work after all."

"Don't give up, your highness," Vanessa snapped. "Mama needs us."

Jace's eyes blazed, and his hand tightened on Derrick's. "I'm not giving up. I'm just saying it like it is. No shade on you, Katy. Cereal's gotta be a bitch to call up from the afterlife."

"I can do it," Katy said. She didn't look at Jace. Her head was tipped back and her eyes closed, a slight wrinkle to her nose. "There's just something… missing…"

Derrick gasped. "It's not balanced. It can't be more than the sum of its parts if it doesn't have all its parts."

Vanessa looked at him, her blue eyes twinkling. "We need the stuff in Mama's basket."

"Excuse me."

As one, the quartet looked up to see Mama standing near the end of the aisle. Her white dress was as prim as ever, and her basket hung from her arm, practically shining with all the pieces she'd managed to gather: the half-gallon of milk, the bottle of orange juice, the carton of eggs, the pack of bacon, and the single, large grapefruit.

She peered at the group with an assessing eye. "You are… looking for Frosty Pops?"

Jace stiffened. Katy went still, too, but in a different way.

Derrick glanced at Vanessa, and she gave him a sharp nod.

He released her hand and held his out to Mama.

"Come join our circle, Mama. We'd really like your help."

Beside him, Jace whispered frantically. "Oh my god. Are you crazy?"

But he didn't try to leave, so Derrick ignored him.

Mama stood where she was a moment longer. Then, hesitantly at first, she came over and knelt at Derrick's side. She daintily slipped her basket from her arm and placed it in the middle beside the candle and the powders. Then she took Derrick's and Vanessa's hands.

Her touch wasn't that cold this time. Derrick only shivered once, then went still.

Katy nodded, then closed her eyes again. "We call upon the spirit of Frosty Pops. Will they come to speak to us?"

This time, when the refrigerators cut off, so did the lights overhead. Their little group was plunged into darkness, with only the flickering candle flame between them to pierce it.

The three powders swirled together, rising into the air above the candle flame to form a cloud. A smell emanated up from the depths below Papa Gerry's 24-hour Green Grocer, a stench first stale, then scorched. A crackling sound, like milk on furious rice puffs, pressed against Derrick's ears as it grew into a roar. A strong urge to vomit rose in his throat.

He swallowed against it and held tight to Mama's and Jace's hands.

"Frosty Pops!" he shouted. "We call you to balance this breakfast!"

A shriek rang out through the grocery store, and a huge, snakelike figure of smoke and shadow rose into the darkness around them. When it moved, it rattled like processed cereal tumbling over itself. As it coalesced, the fragments of its body became visible: a hundred thousand compressed balls of wheat, corn, and maybe a little bit of rice, all tinged in highly artificial yellow. All coated with an unhealthy slather of white, sugary, tooth-rotting glaze.

Frosty Pops had indeed come to their call, but its spirit was vengeful, full of rage at its untimely, fiery demise. It would not be tamed to its bowl.

They'd summoned a cereal demon.

Double Hex Katy leapt into action. She broke the circle, dropping Vanessa's and Jace's hands and swiping the candle up from the floor. Then she spun to face the demon, candle and free hand lifted.

"In the name of the maiden, the mother, and the crone, we command you to balance this breakfast!" she shouted. With her free hand, she sketched sigils in the air.

The demon screamed at her, spraying flecks of shredded wheat in her face. Katy didn't flinch. She kept drawing her sigils.

Then the demon rushed her.

"Katy!" Derrick shouted.

Granules of Frosty Pops flew everywhere like ocean spray as the demon plowed into her. The candle snuffed out, and

Katy let out a cry, which was quickly muffled by the cascade of cereal. Shelves wobbled, then toppled backwards into aisle six with a deafening crash.

"Oh, my," said Mama. Her body was fading into her more see-through, ghostly state, and her shoulders were pulled in as if in fear.

"Oh, hell no," said Vanessa. She was on her feet and running towards the demon as it drew itself back to strike at Katy again. She leaped, one leg kicked forward, the other tucked up and under. Her twin ponytails fluttered behind her like black silken streamers. The hem of her obscure band t-shirt lifted, exposing the twining rose and thorn tattoo that spread across the small of her back.

Derrick could have sworn the scene went into slow-mo for real.

The thick, hard sole of her high-laced goth boot slammed into the Frosty Pop demon's head, knocking it away from Katy with an audible crunch.

"I don't care what your complaint is," Vanessa said when she landed, panting. "Nobody gets away with screaming at my employees."

Time sped up again as the demon shook itself. Bits and pieces of broken cereal scattered across the linoleum, and the fallen shelves banged together with the demon's movement. Katy scrambled to her feet, her hands moving frantically to form more sigils.

But the demon had turned its attention to Vanessa now. The cereal that made up its body glowed like embers. Wisps of smoke curled up to cloud the ceiling and choke the fools who had summoned it.

Derrick readied himself to throw his entire hulk upon the over-processed monster, but first he glanced side to side to see what had become of Mama or Jace. He didn't want to leave them unprotected in his haste to rescue Vanessa.

He found himself standing alone.

Anger and worry meshed within him, but he didn't have time to sort any of that out. The demon was lunging for Vanessa, jaws open and burnt-flour reek pouring forth. Vanessa stumbled backwards, one arm held across her face to block the stench.

Derrick flew forward to grapple the demon.

Holding a being of free-flowing cereal was not as easy as pinning a human teenaged boy. No matter where he grabbed, the thing flowed away from him. But he didn't give up. The thing's attention was on him, now, and he squatted into a stance that would keep his center of gravity low as he circled the demon, waiting for an opportunity.

Back and forth he shuffled, and the Frosty Pops demon shifted and twisted. Now the shelves on the aisle eight side toppled, victims of the monster's lashing tail. The demon flashed forward, jaws crunching as Derrick dodged away and behind it.

He leapt onto its back, wrapping his arms and legs around it wherever he could.

Full Nelson, he thought. *Or something like it.*

Sticky sugar glaze coated his fingers, his arms, and his jeans. In his grip, the demon thrashed and shrieked loud enough the darkened fluorescent bulbs overhead cracked. The cereal began shifting again, trying to get out of Derrick's hold.

Derrick held on, but his heart sank with every Frosty Pop that slid against his skin.

"Derrick!" Vanessa yelled. She was below, holding Double Hex Katy up as the younger girl slumped in exhaustion. The light in Vanessa's blue eyes said she wanted to fight on, but the shake of her head said she had to tap out.

The cereal shifted again. Derrick held on tight as he could.

Then, a crackle came over the in-store loudspeaker system. A voice, high and dark, spoke in a strange lilting meter.

> *A coldness before me*
> *and a crunch, so fresh*
> *aligns with*
> *a savor of bacon*

Jace. Reading his deep, dark poetry out over the speakers for the whole store to hear. He stood over at the pole where the telephone hung, holding the handpiece so the receiver was at his mouth and the earpiece lay against his shoulder.

His other hand stretched behind him, where Mama held it as she crooned words of support.

"That's so beautiful, Jace," she said. "Read some more."

The demon froze, all its pieces staying put for one tiny moment of surprise.

That moment was long enough. Derrick readjusted his grip and got the thing into a headlock.

Instantly, the demon fought back, hissing and jerking hard enough Derrick's arms almost wrenched out of their sockets.

Derrick didn't think the poem was really all that good, but

what the hell did he know? All he really knew was that in Jace's hesitant lull, the cereal demon had regained enough power to get *this close* to thrashing his nards to pulp.

"Keep reading!" he shouted.

The speakers crackled again.

> *Behold! A missing*
> *piece is found*
> *A start bright*
> *and strong with the flavor of love*

The demon shuddered. Its shrieks became coughs which belched forth more smoke. Derrick tried to breathe through his mouth as he kept his hold. The demon was sinking towards the floor. He almost had it pinned.

"Go, Jace!" said Katy. "Bind it!"

Jace, now nodding as he spoke his words, stepped forward so the pole was no longer between him and the monster he was subduing. His voice grew strong for the final stanza.

Behind him, Mama beamed.

> *And my heart, once*
> *black and hollow*
> *hungers*
> *for this offered balance*

The demon was on the floor now. Derrick's weight was enough to keep it pinned as it whimpered and whined. The smell of burnt cereal was fading.

Mama strode forward, as prim as ever, and picked up the

wooden bowl from where it still sat amongst the mess of flour, corn starch, and sugar. Then she stepped up to the demon's collapsing head.

"Now, then. I'm asking you nicely *one last time* to please balance this breakfast. Don't make me count to three."

She held the bowl out expectantly.

The demon wriggled and let out a rattly sound of protest.

"One."

The demon gathered its scattered self sulkily and huffed like a toddler. If Derrick weren't holding it, it would have turned its back on her. It didn't think Mama would really punish it.

Mama simply pressed the bowl closer to it. "*Two.*"

The demon tried to push away, but Derrick didn't let it.

Mama's hair began to rise around her, and her face took on a resigned expression as it hollowed out. "Thr—"

With a fearful yip, the demon — the Frosty Pops — poured themselves out of Derrick's grip and into the bowl. The tinkling chime of them filling it rippled through aisle seven. Along with that sound came also the sizzling of bacon, the cracking of eggs, and the pouring of milk and OJ. A snick of a knife halved a grapefruit.

All at once, the lights in the store came back on, no longer harsh fluorescent, but warm, homey light that evoked a sunrise.

Mama stood beside the dining table in the middle of the wreckage of aisle seven and smiled down at her perfect breakfast with her hands clutched against her breast. Tears glistened in her eyes.

"Oh," she said. "*Frosty Pops.*"

"Holy fuck, we did it," Jace said. He'd hung up the phone and come to stand with Vanessa and Katy, sliding his own shoulder under Katy's so Vanessa could rest, but Vanessa kept her arm around Katy in a sisterly hug.

Derrick slowly got to his feet. His muscles felt well-used and ready to stretch. Rolling his shoulders and wrists, he wiped his sugar-coated hands on his jeans and went to join his coworkers.

For a moment, they all grinned at one another like idiots. Then Jace nodded towards the table. "She's still here, though. Didn't we calm her restless spirit? We got her her Frosty Pops."

Derrick looked. Sure enough, Mama stood beside the table still, waiting.

"They're not for her," he said.

Mama nodded. "They're the best way for a kid to start the day. All the vitamins and nutrients a growing kid needs. I know you all have big days coming up, don't you? So I made sure to put together a breakfast that will give you a great start."

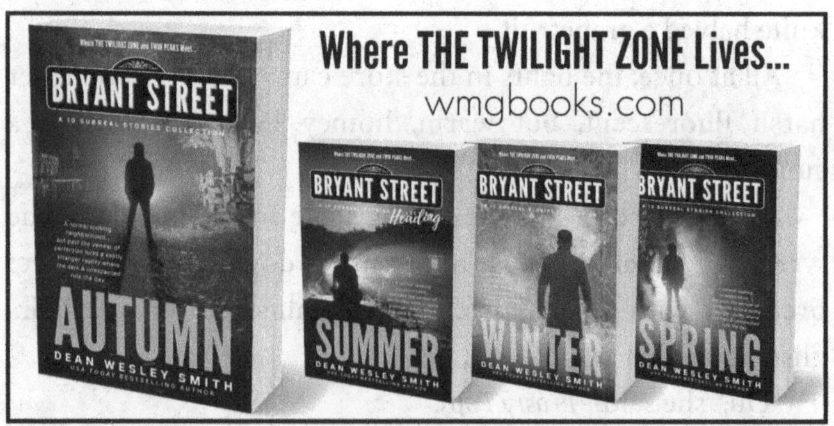

"Oh, hell," said Jace.

Vanessa elbowed him, lightly. "Be polite, or I'll make you go clean your toilets again while the rest of us have breakfast."

All together, the four of them descended on the table.

From the first bite, the food was all so delicious Derrick thought *he* might try his hand at poetry. The bacon was exactly as crispy as he liked it, the OJ was tart and fresh, the eggs jammy and steaming, the grapefruit sweet.

And the Frosty Pops, well…

They just balanced everything.

Derrick leaned back in his chair, satisfied. He smiled around the table at his Papa Gerry's family, and they all smiled back at him. Then, he turned to look over his shoulder. "Thanks, Mama. That was great."

But Mama wasn't there.

Katy tipped her head to one side. "She's moved on now. Her business is finished."

"Well," Vanessa said, pushing her chair back with a squeal. "These shelves aren't going to pick themselves back up. Come on, up and at 'em."

Jace groaned, and Katy stuck her tongue out at him. But they worked together to right the first shelf while Derrick did the second by himself.

"Way to go, Muscles," said Vanessa.

Derrick grinned.

Still, before the air truly cleared of all spiritual presence, Derrick could have sworn he felt the ghostly touch of a pair of lips on his forehead and an arm across his shoulders.

Mama would always believe in him.

THE DAY before the fall semester started, Derrick made his way to the little hallway outside the store manager's office. He'd put it off as long as he could, but the time had come. He had to change his shift if he wanted to attend his morning classes with the proper energy. And, given the talk he'd had with his academic advisor yesterday in which he'd officially changed his major from Undecided to English, he definitely wanted to focus on his studies.

But when he got there, he found Double Hex Katy coming out the door.

"Hey," she said, smiling a little. "I just quit."

"Really? Is that good?"

"Yeah. I'm going back to high school." She laughed, and it was quiet, but confident.

"Nice! You'll kill it."

"Thanks. I feel… ready, I guess. I can handle the other kids, even if they bully me."

"Hey, you know who to ask if you need someone to be a meat shield."

Double Hex Katy cast him a look that told him he was overplaying it. Then she stepped past him, waving in a goodbye sigil.

Jace strolled up as she left. He had his hands in his pockets and his Papa Gerry's vest on. His eyebrow piercing sparkled in the fluorescent lights as he frowned at the paper in Derrick's hand. "Man, is everyone leaving? I'm gonna be all on my lonesome on night shift. Who'll shoo all the losers out of the back room when it's time to restock?"

Derrick blinked. "Vanessa quit, too?"

"She asked to be switched to day shift, even though it meant taking a demotion from shift leader. I think she's planning on taking night classes or something. You two will get to be all cozy together, I guess. At least, if you ever get up the nerve to ask her out, loser."

He said it with a smile.

Derrick chuckled. "I guess that means you've got night shift seniority. Doesn't that make you Shift Leader Jace?"

"Ah, hell. I suppose that means coven-shooing duty falls to my lot."

"Try not to enjoy it too much."

"Ha ha," Jace said. He turned to stroll back down the hallway to the main store. But then he paused and glanced back.

"Hey, so. There's this open mic night at that one coffee shop up on campus. I'm thinking of going. Maybe reading some of my stuff."

"When is it? I'll be there."

Jace shared the info, and the two of them fist-bumped to seal the deal.

Then Derrick met with the manager.

When he walked out into the back alley, fresh part-time day shift schedule in hand, she was there, leaning against the brick of the little nook opposite the dumpster. Shift Leader no longer; now only Vanessa. Her hair was in a single braid today, pulled over the front of her band t-shirt.

"Hey, I think I've heard of them," Derrick said as he approached.

She quirked a half smile up at him. "Yeah, they had a song

that went somewhat mainstream. But all their best work is the stuff no one's heard of."

"Figures."

Vanessa kicked one high-laced boot out and tapped Derrick lightly on his shin. "So, Muscles. Coworker," she said. "Wanna catch a movie tonight? I hear the theater on the other side of campus has a ghost that turns up to watch old Audrey Hepburn films."

"A romantic, then," Derrick said as his chest threatened to burst. *Yes*, he celebrated internally. *Hell yes.*

"We could grab dinner after," he said. "I know a great place that serves breakfast 24/7."

START HERE

DivingintotheWreck.com

LISA SILVERTHORNE

Acclaimed veteran fantasy and science fiction writer Lisa Silverthorne can set a scene early better than anyone I have read. In this story, when the body sloshes onto the table, I am hooked.

And Lisa never disappoints.

Lisa sells her fantastic short fiction to many, many markets, including just this last holiday a couple stories to the Holiday Spectacular.

For a lot more about Lisa's stories and her growing new Game of Lost Souls series, and other new fantasy series, plus the beautiful covers she designs, go to http://www.lisasilverthorne.com/

RENA 733

LISA SILVERTHORNE

There wasn't much left of #733. Hardly enough to bury, much less autopsy. Another dead soldier from the multitude of colonization squadrons. I snapped on my rubber gloves, hating this job, and peeled back the body bag flaps.

I never called the soldiers by anything other than their tag number, but this one was so young – no more than twenty. Seeing another half-faced, burned body made me ill. I couldn't help myself, the name Rena just popped into my head. Her one eye, green, stared strangely content past me as I sloshed her remains onto the chrome table. Stale blood scent mixed with germicide. I scanned the reclamation orders on the side of the bag with a light pen: recover one microfeed and one MRC. A memory replacement chip. My hands began to shake.

I shifted Rena 733's body toward the small image capture scanner at the edge of the table. The red light winked on and encircled her head, gathering streams of data from the MRC. The scanner hummed, converting the raw data into an enhanced viewable format. EVF produced a third person video effect of the stored memories. The data could only be converted to EVF once. In a few moments, a summary scan of the chip, only the last 48 hours of this soldier's life, would be played back on the screen above my head. Sometimes, MRCs were damaged by the extraction, so this prescan was a failsafe. The HQ suits had to have their data.

The autopsy room door slid open and medtech student, Deanna Fitzsimmons entered the chamber. Her bobbed blonde hair lay flat against her pale cheeks and thin face. This was Deanna's first week at the station and already, she reminded me a lot of myself back in medical school. It had been more than a year since I last worked with a partner. Deanna's face contorted when she glanced at the body on the table.

"Another one?" She inhaled sharply. "That's the fifteenth casualty since lunch. Don't you get tired of this, doctor?"

I leaned against the table, studying Deanna's tired blue eyes and the fine lines beginning around her nose and mouth. She wasn't much older than Rena 733. I hated throwing so many cases at her in her first week, but she'd have to get used to dealing with the bodies.

"I don't think I can look at another one today," I said, surprised by the weariness in my voice. I knew Deanna couldn't handle another autopsy like this one today. "Why don't you take log duty this time?"

Deanna smiled, relieved by my suggestion. She turned away from the table and picked up the datapad that hung on the far wall. She scrolled through the chart and her gaze snapped up, looking past Rena 733 – even past me.

"Ready whenever you are, Dr. Kingston."

"Good," I said. "We'll begin as soon as the data capture is complete."

"When do you match tags with names?"

"I don't. They handle that back on Earth," I answered. And for that, I was thankful.

I glanced up, seeing the blank screen, then flicked on the autopsy laser. Deanna flinched at the sound. The chrome fixtures cast the scanner's red sheen against the shiny gray, tiled walls and floor. Deanna walked over to the space station portal as I cut open Rena 733's cranium.

Voices echoed through the chamber and I looked up to see desert stretching into velvet, umber hills on the view screen, the horizon a mixture of creams and rust. The barrel of Rena 733's Stupor plasma rifle, slung over one shoulder, bobbed at the edge of the view screen.

Twenty. I cringed, gazing from Rena 733's burned face to

Deanna's pale profile. I remembered being twenty once. Before medical school. Before the Antaris War. Before computer retroviruses crippled the nets and we lost most of our private technology to the government. I sighed. Before MRCs. Hundreds of soldiers had come through this station, but until today, it had never bothered me. Only another report to upload. Still, I wondered if it was Deanna or the MRC that disturbed me most.

I reached up to shut off the output. I didn't want to know anymore than I had to – it just made my job harder.

"What are you doing?" Deanna asked.

"Shutting off the MRC's output."

Deanna frowned. "Don't you want to know who she was?"

I shook my head and looked away from the screen.

"But why? She's out there protecting our world. She should be given more respect than a number."

I set down the laser. "Do you really understand what an MRC is?" I asked, knowing at best, she'd only read about them.

"It records –"

I shook my head. "No, Deanna, it *parses*. It selectively parses out memories and feeds back only the ones that pass the algorithm. Anything that causes adverse emotional reactions to the job is quickly and permanently parsed out."

Deanna's face whitened. "God. How horrible."

"The parsed out memories remain on the chip, so HQ can access them. But she can't. I don't want to invade her privacy."

Reaching up to the screen, I laid my hand against the shut off switch, but something made me stop. "Are you sure you want to see this? I don't."

She had that passerby look on her face, that mixture of revulsion and unblinking curiosity that people displayed at the scene of a tragedy. Finally, she nodded. "In case she had a last request or something," she said in a small voice.

I pulled my hand away, dreading the playback. Only once had I allowed myself to watch one of these before.

On the screen, another soldier crouched beside Rena 733, his sandy hair tousled and his face sweaty. He examined claw-like footprints, dipping a gloved hand into the fine, gold sand. "No sign of them, Gates," said the man. "Continue tracking or return to camp?"

"Are we seeing through her eyes?" Deanna asked.

"Sort of. The many layers of images and points of view are brought together so we see this soldier as well as what she saw and felt."

"Her name's Gates," said Deanna.

I sighed. Yes, she was right. Rena 733 had a real name, but in her present state, I found that fact too painful.

"They can't be far, Ryan," Gates answered in a smooth, alto voice. "The Colonel wants a position report before 19:00."

"Until we find our patrol's insides strung out like streamers, those Antaran bastards won't show themselves."

"Shut up, Ryan," Gates said and squinted at the horizon. Her thoughts whispered through the speakers, the tone softer and echoing due to the computer enhancement of her thoughts.

I tried not to watch the screen, but I couldn't help myself.

What if we do find them? What then? I'm not afraid and I should be. Why do I want so desperately to go after the Antarans like this? I even dream about it. I want to come out here and fight...

except when I'm here. What's the matter with me? Gates rubbed her face and gripped the rifle tighter.

"She doesn't know," I said in a half-whisper, my mouth falling open. "My God, they put those things in her head and didn't even tell her."

Ryan stood up, brushing the sand off his beige uniform. "Gates? Do you ever – no, forget it," he said, waving her off.

She frowned and turned toward him. "What? Do I ever what?"

He gazed down at the ground, parting the sand into a semi-circle with the toe of his boot. "Do you ever . . . well, fear these encounters?"

"Sometimes. Do you?"

He nodded. "I feel like pissing my pants right now."

Why aren't I that scared? She pointed toward a bluff in the distance. "We'll hike out to there and go back to base if we turn up nothing."

"Agreed," said Ryan, who shoved his rifle back over his shoulder.

Gates moved in front of him, her boots whisking across the sand, but Ryan's scream forced her to turn – too late. Talons blurred. A spiky appendage burst up from the sand, piercing Ryan's body. He screamed again. Sliding the plasma rifle into her hands, Gates squeezed off a volley of blasts into the sand until something screeched. The appendage splattered into an inky puddle beside Ryan's crumpled body.

She collapsed beside him and pulled him up from the ground, one arm balancing the plasma rifle that quivered at the edge of the view screen. He wheezed, blood dripping from his nose and mouth, intestines dangling from his torso. He grabbed her sleeve.

Oh, God. Don't die on me! Please don't die! "Hang on, Ryan — I got you!"

"Gates, I – Gates – " His hand fell away from her sleeve.

"Sssh, don't talk now." *Why Ryan? Why! We went through boot camp together.* Her hushed voice reverberated again. *Oh, God, he's dying.*

I turned away when Gates began to sob, the rawness in her voice grating.

"My God," said Deanna. "Her best friend just got killed!" She let the datapad fall onto a countertop and she looked away from the screen.

"They're both at peace now," I offered.

"At peace? He was ripped apart and she was blown to pieces!"

I studied Deanna's reddening face, the tears rimming her eyes. "Death is a part of life and we have to accept that. You have to accept that if you're going to be a Frontline Tech."

The anger twisting her features surprised me. She didn't even know these people.

"And you need to understand that when you open those bags, there are people inside – not numbers."

"That's why this job never gets easier," I said, turning toward Rena 733, and picked up the tissue-resin separator from the instrument tray.

My stomach ached when I sifted through the remains of Rena 733's cerebrum and midbrain for the microfeed. The nanoprocessor-controlled microfeed was activated by combat and controlled aggression and its effects – adrenalin rushes, endorphin releases. I shook my head. Poor kid was addicted to battle. Kept her out there fighting just to feel good. Craving the kill like some psychopath. This was the third soldier I had seen beta-testing these new combat enhancements.

"Make a note on the chart that Rena 733 is another combat technology beta-tester, Fitzsimmons."

"All this technology and yet this war goes on forever," said Deanna, not diverting her gaze from the view screen. She didn't even look at the datapad as she typed.

She was right. Too many people were dying and with every territory we gained, we lost one somewhere else. It was a stalemate at best. When I was a first year, I had Deanna's idealism. I remember standing at the armed forces's recruitment desk, fresh out of med school on a mission of mercy. I wanted to go to the front and save lives. Back then, like Gates, I didn't know the cost. Didn't even understand it. Not sure I did now.

Busying myself with the extractions, I shut out the view screen's sounds of shifting sand as Gates carried Ryan back to camp. I found the ATP-driven microfeed lodged in Rena's brain stem. It had been surgically implanted high into her brain's third ventricle, but whatever explosive she had stepped on must have caused the microfeed to dislodge and pierce the brain stem.

As I probed deeper, I found that some bastard surgeon had removed her amygdalae so she couldn't develop a fear of the enemy. Even the hippocampus had been altered, an MRC attached to it. I shuddered at the sight of the tiny, black chip containing all her memories. It hijacked her ability to form new ones, storing all of them into the chip and then selectively parsing out everything but the harmless memories for transmission. Working with the tissue-resin separator, I carefully dislodged the microfeed.

I watched as Gates entered her base camp and then her barracks. Abruptly, the screen went dark, the computer parsing out sleep and dream sequences. I sighed. Gates only had twenty-four hours left. Twenty years old with twenty-four hours to live.

The screen suddenly blurred to daylight, Gates fumbling out of her barracks in full field gear. One of the other soldiers approached.

"Sorry to hear about Ryan, Heather," said the soldier, shaking her head. "Tough break. I know how close you two were."

"What are you talking about?" Gates asked.

"I heard about the ambush yesterday. I'm really sorry."

What's she talking about? I didn't hear about any ambush. There was a Ryan in boot camp, but not out here. She's been offworld too long. "Right – thanks," Gates mumbled. "When do we frag the Antaris camp?"

I gripped the edge of the table. That bastard chip had even parsed out Ryan's existence. It didn't even leave her a memory of her best friend.

The other soldier checked her watch. "T minus six hours. We have to wait for an orbit window. Can't go in with those satellites firing at us and our shuttle cover."

I extracted the memory replacement chip and mumbled through my own personal damage assessment, accounting for lost limbs, obliterated organs, and cause of death. Too bad "blown to bits" wasn't anywhere on my medical ROMs. Her legs and half her chest were gone. The only real thing left of Rena 733, the only thing that contained anything that was once her, was the memory replacement chip. It contained Rena 733's entire career as a soldier – and her last days. To the government, it was only beta test data and now the suits would see it all, whether she had wanted them to or not.

"Open computer log. Autopsy #733, Dr. Jeannette Kingston presiding, Deanna Fitzsimmons assisting."

For the computer log, I rolled off a string of observations, "Enhancement of reticular formation still intact, limbic system remained functional at time of death . . ." For the government report that would be core-dumped into some net info tomb.

"So, when you going home, Gates," asked a voice from the view screen. I turned around again, seeing Gates marching beside a weather-beaten soldier with haggard gray eyes.

"End of the month they tell me. Guess my tour's up. I'll miss it." *And that scares me. I miss Mom and Dad. Haven't even seen my new niece yet, but leaving the troop scares the hell out of me. Makes me feel sick. What will I do?*

My eyes misted. That new niece was probably in school now, but she didn't know that. More memories stolen, parsed away by the MRC. It was all stored in the chip, but she couldn't access it. My hands began to shake again. They didn't even let her remember her best friend beyond boot camp. Couldn't let a soldier form attachments. When one died, that memory was parsed into the bit bucket. Soldiers couldn't care about anything out here. Neither could doctors. What had they done to this girl? Gates was hard around the edges, addicted to combat, and unafraid of an enemy that had shredded her to ribbons. The suits had made her into some animal with its instinct removed. How many soldiers had they done this to? But this soldier was different now; she had a name, emotions – a family.

I set down the tissue-resin separator, the distant memory of a little girl brought into emergency once when I was in residency. She had drowned in a swimming pool when her father had left her alone in the backyard. They had revived her en route, but she died before I could even tube her. Where had that memory come from? I hadn't thought about that in years. My eyes filled with tears. In medical school, one of my professors had warned me that there'd be a handful of cases that would stay with me. I guess this was one of those cases.

Biting my lip, I tried not to look at Rena 733's face, but I couldn't stop myself. In the remains of her face, I saw that child's desperate, pleading green eyes suddenly turn dull, the monitor flat-lining with a screech. I had just stood there, the endotracheal tube dangling from my hand. Dammit, it wasn't supposed to be this way here. That's why they all had numbers and no names. It was too hard when they had names – and pasts. I looked away from Rena 733's half-face and with shaking hands, I picked up the tissue-resin separator again. Why couldn't I stop shaking?

Suddenly, I felt Rena 733's blood on my gloves. Hopes and dreams ran through it. Anger and tears. Twenty years' worth. Like Deanna. Rena 733 was more than bone to cut through or blood needed for typing and DNA extraction. She was more than autopsy #733.

Carefully, I laid the memory replacement chip in a tray beside the microfeed. Moving to the processing equipment to the right of the table, I sent the chip through. The instrument whirred and groaned, converting all the information into its final enhanced viewable format. All the suits required now was a viewer and they could access all Gates's memories.

On the view screen, Heather Gates screamed as the ground exploded beneath her, throwing her several meters across the sand. For an instant, she survived the blast. Her gaze traveled up to the sky. "Mom, I need you," she gurgled, but in a moment, the view screen winked out and the processing unit stopped. The summary scan had concluded. Heather Gates's life was over.

"They'll see it all, won't they?" Deanna asked in a small voice. "And she won't even know about it. It isn't fair."

I picked up the chip from the tray. Gates's entire soldiering career lay on this chip, private moments, personal feelings belonging only to Heather Gates. And so much of it had been cut off from her memory. Cheated away from her by this MRC.

"You're right, Deanna," I said. "It isn't fair."

I dropped the little memory prison onto the table. Part of Gates' life had been in my hands, like that little girl's had been and all those soldiers on the front line. Case numbers blurred with blood types and bar codes as I picked up a wide-handled clamp. Those soldiers had lives before they came to me. Heather Gates did too and so did I once.

"Computer, pause autopsy record #733."

Slamming the clamp handle against the MRC, I pounded it and pounded it until it was shards of resin and silicon. The crunching of the silicon filled the silence and I cherished the sound. It wasn't bone splitting or a body bag unzipping. It was my anger and there was nothing the government could do about it. Deanna stood frozen beside the table, her mouth gaping.

"If Heather Gates wasn't allowed to remember these things, then the government won't get the privilege either."

"Computer, resume autopsy record #733. Note: MRC did not survive the blast. Only shards detected throughout the cortex and cerebrum. Fragments will follow under separate cover. End record. End report." I motioned toward Deanna. "Send the report, please."

While Deanna uploaded the report, I gathered the MRC fragments into a small container. Heather Gates' memories would stay her own – for however long she had them. It was the only shred of dignity I could offer her now.

I barcoded the cause of death information into a label that I printed and attached to the body bag. I didn't need to see a view screen to know how she died. After microsuturing the remains of Gates back together, I laid her to rest in the body bag.

I zipped up the body bag and then laid a hand against my neck, knowing that tomorrow I wouldn't remember Heather Gates or my conversation with Deanna. Heather Gates would be #733 again. "Doctor Kingston," said Deanna, her voice soft. "I've been wanting to ask – why did you call her Rena?"

"Computer, scan KingstonJL."

I closed my eyes as the white scan light slid across me.

"Why are you doing that?" Deanna asked.

"Display report on screen." I pointed to the computer view screen. "Read it, Deanna."

"Why?" she asked, shaking her head.

"Just read it."

Her gaze flitted across the data and I read it with her. Every day, it was new to me, too. Finally, she gasped and her gaze jerked toward me. Tears welled in my eyes.

"You've got an MRC."

I NODDED. "This job required it. I used to write myself notes when I got out of the hospital, so I wouldn't forget anything. Now, I just append them into my login scripts."

"Why didn't you turn down the job?" Her eyes were wide.

"Turn it down?" I laughed bitterly. "I volunteered for it!"

"You volunteered?"

"I thought it would be better than dying inside every time a soldier died." Or a child. I leaned against the table. "Better than crying my heart out for months and months after a child died in my arms. I thought working with numbers would be easier. That way I wouldn't die inside. I didn't know the MRC was just another way to die." And I didn't know the government would take away memories they had no right to take.

The silence was palpable and I wanted to reach out and shove it aside. Deanna could only stare at me, a tear funneling down her cheek.

"I'm so sorry," she finally whispered.

"Every morning, when I log into the system, I play back a history file that I create every night. But it isn't enough. Words on a screen meant for someone else. I'm living in the third person, Deanna."

I laid my hand on the body bag, wanting to exchange places with Heather Gates.

Deanna walked over to me and squeezed my arm. "It's all right, doctor. You don't have to answer my question."

I felt the sobs ache through me, my knees trembling with weakness. "But I do. Rena was the name of my daughter, Rena Diane Kingston. She would have been twenty-one this month." I sucked in a deep breath. "She drowned when she was two. When I finished my residency, the government thought it best to parse out her memory – without my consent. When I took this job, I didn't know they would take away my daughter's memory."

"How . . . did you find out?"

I picked up a shard of the MRC left behind on the examination table. "Their algorithm cleaned my memories of Rena, but their chip couldn't totally parse my child from my thoughts. It only pushed her back until she became a nameless child in ER. It was the best the bastards could do. But they missed one thing."

Deanna stared at me for a moment. "What was that?" she said finally in a soft voice.

"My ex-husband. I lost track of him when he joined the Service until – " I sighed. "Until he came through here. And it was all there in his MRC, my daughter, the accident, the divorce – everything."

Deanna shook her head. "But your memory would have been –"

"Parsed out? Most of it, maybe, but not out of my login script. What happened to her and who she was will always be there – every time I log in."

Pressing against the MRC shard, I snapped it between my fingers and let the pieces fall to the floor. I would remember and mourn my daughter whether they let me or not. Rena Diane Kingston. She had a name again and I would remember it.

POKER BOY

Read all his adventures at

wmgbooks.com

ROBERT JESCHONEK

With this month's featured story, Robert Jeschonek continues his streak of being in every issue of this magazine. All thirty-two plus Issue Zero.

The reason Robert has this streak is simply because his stories are often just perfect Pulphouse stories. Take this story, for example. His main character is coherent gamma radiation on the surface of a green star and it goes from there. Have fun!

Robert's stories have appeared in dozens of magazines and he has published dozens of novels as well. He has even worked for DC Comics and early in his career sold me a couple stories when I was editing for Star Trek at Pocket Books. He seems to be able to do it all. And to see all the amazing projects he has done, check out his website at https://www.robertjeschonek.com/

KITTY ON A HOT, DYING STAR

ROBERT JESCHONEK

I had just about finished my work on the surface of the green sun, Ardora, when I heard about the impossible vibration that was living not far away.

Riding a blanket of radio waves, I set out, determined to detect this vibration for myself. The radio blanket made the trip a little smoother though Ardora was storming, throwing off salvos of charged particles that made travel rough even for a field of coherent gamma radiation like me.

Gliding over the swirling emerald flames, I wondered what I would find of this vibration. So many thoughtful bursts and waves had told of the miracle and mystery of its existence. I could not resist delving further, in spite of my need to get away from this green star quickly.

The fact was, Ardora would soon be gone, and with it every burst and wave and vibration that inhabited its sizzling surface. Within days, perhaps hours, this mighty sun would disappear from the firmament, collapsing into a massive black hole.

It was something I couldn't bear to witness again.

As I soared over a vast channel through the chromosphere, alive with a river of roiling green flame, I admired the spectacular beauty of Ardora. It was no wonder I'd come here long ago to bask in its glories—to immerse my own special pattern in their midst.

I hadn't known then that it was coming to an end…and saving its secrets would become the work of many years. That capturing the greatest treasures of its inhabitants—their stories and songs—would be the finest thing I'd ever do.

I saw some of those inhabitants below me now, waving as I passed—flashing tongues of atomic fire, bound by bands of magnetic force. They were among the people of Ardora, trillions in number, minds woven of energetic particles and strings twirling deep in the quantum foam. When the sun died, it would take them with it.

It didn't have to be that way…but the Ardorans loved their home so much, they were *choosing* to die with it. They would never know if escape was possible, because they'd decided not even to try. They were willing to throw their lives and everything special about them out the window, leaving no trace to be remembered by the other civilized races of the galaxy.

At least, that was what would have happened if I hadn't learned of the coming threat and dedicated my expertise to preserving the Ardorans' stories and songs…if I hadn't saved them in coded bursts of x-rays and radio waves and shot them into space, the product of billions of interviews with multitudes of special people.

And yet, it seemed, I'd missed one.

This should not have surprised me. I soon realized, as I followed the directions my sources had given me, that the terrain became increasingly difficult to navigate in this part of Ardora—a remote area churning with mega-powerful nuclear explosions. The resulting turbulence tossed me like a helium atom in a solar flare, sending me spinning to the point of disorientation.

Just as I fought my way through the worst of the blasts, an unexpected gale of spacetime distortion nearly tore me apart. It took everything I could do to keep my waves united and prevent my consciousness from disintegrating.

As I did, I thought of Xynth, another star whose destruction I'd witnessed up close. I remembered how the turbulence of its late-stage upheaval had nearly shredded me, how it had left me whirling in a state of mindless helplessness. It had taken a seeming eternity to return to consciousness—and my failure to launch a rescue operation more quickly had cost my research team their lives. Four great minds had been lost in the star-death of Xynth.

I could *never* forgive myself for that...but at least it wouldn't happen exactly the same way this time. I hadn't teamed with researchers on Ardora; since the disaster on Xynth, I'd insisted on working alone, leaving other professionals out of it.

Not having to worry about teammates was a relief, freeing me to concentrate on my own survival. Even as I emerged from the spacetime gale, however, a massive column of fire surged past, stunning me with its unbelievable heat and light. It just missed carrying me off into space, though it left me momentarily senseless.

As the shock faded, I saw I'd entered a region of calm, the eye of the storm. Believing I'd reached my destination, I looked around.

But when I saw what awaited below, I wondered if I'd found something else entirely. Something far stranger and less explicable than an errant vibration.

A figure looked up at me. It appeared to be some kind of creature, standing upright, with a head, two upper appendages, and two lower ones, all connected to a central trunk. It had some kind of pale pink skin, draped with a flowing white garment.

It seemed to be organic, this creature. I'd seen such life-forms on planets and moons before, in this solar system and elsewhere...but never *here*. Never somewhere they should not have been able to exist.

Never on the roiling, searing surface of a *sun*.

———

PATTERNS OF CURIOSITY overpowered my wavelengths. My guard was up, but I couldn't resist getting closer, finding out more.

It was then, as I slowly descended toward the creature, that I realized it could see me. It looked right in my direction, raised an upper appendage, and waved it back and forth—meanwhile calling out, projecting a sonic vibration from an orifice—a maw, a mouth—on the lower part of its head.

"Hello there!" Even with the green-flamed blast furnace of Ardora roaring around me, I somehow heard the creature's sounds clearly. "Very good to meet you, friend!"

Not only that, but I somehow made *sense* of those sounds. I understood them as units of spoken language, as words, and I knew what they meant.

"Come on down." The creature gestured with its upper appendage, reaching out and curling it back toward itself. "Don't be shy."

I slipped closer, then hesitated…then flowed closer still. I stopped not far from the creature, hovering at a distance that was perhaps equal to twice its full height.

"My name is Kitty Fisher." The features on the front of the creature's head shifted—its eyes widening, its mouth curving up at the corners. "I'm from a place called London, England, though I'm not quite sure how I came to be *here*."

I watched and listened patiently, not really grasping the full context of what the creature was telling me. Where was this *London, England*, anyway? There were sectors of Ardora I'd never been to. Perhaps London was in one of those?

"I'm just hoping someone will tell me how to go home." Kitty reached up and patted the wave of glossy dark brown fibers flowing over its head and upper body. "This place is lovely enough, but it's *ever* so hot."

I followed the words surprisingly well for someone who had never communicated via word units expressed as sound waves before. My general understanding deepened, so not only did the meanings of this new language make basic sense to me, but I knew the creature was female by gender—a *she*, not an *it*.

If only I could respond in a way she'd understand.

"So what can you tell me, good sir?" asked Kitty. "What pearls of wisdom to share out here in the brightest light that ever was, in the year of our Lord 1765?"

Body waves floating on the superheated thermals gusting from below, I stared at her, wishing I could answer.

"Oh, please sir," said Kitty. "I suppose you may be a trifle *starstruck*, given who I am and all, but I assure you, there's no need to keep schtum. If we could speak freely, we might both of us arrive at an understanding."

What do you want, Kitty Fisher? The question rippled from me as all expressions do, as subtle variations in the wavelengths of my fields. It should have taken another sentient radiation flare or a conscious nuclear flame or clutch of time and space and gravity waves to hear what I'd said, let alone comprehend it.

Why, then, did she seem not only to hear me, but to answer my question?

"I have always wanted to be the biggest star ever." Again, her mouth curled up at the corners. "Now look at me." She spread her upper appendages wide, taking in her broiling surroundings. "It would seem I am actually *on* a star."

She made a strange sound in the tubular structure connecting her head to her trunk—a high-pitched, stuttering exhalation of breath like the repeated bursts from a pocket of nuclear steam boiling off Ardora. It went on for a moment, growing louder, and she bent over, eyes pinched shut.

When she straightened and looked at me again, her eyes

twinkled with moisture like the dew wicking from a comet melting in a stream of solar wind.

"Do you want to know the funniest part?" she said. "Now that I'm *here*, a *star* on an actual *star*, all I want to do is go home!"

WHAT DID you mean about being a star? I asked the question in my usual tongue, as fluctuations of my radiation wavelengths. *You don't look like any star I've ever seen.*

At first, she didn't look at me, and I worried that my message hadn't gotten through. The communication we shared seemed impossible at best...though no more so than her very presence on the superheated surface of Ardora.

But then, Kitty started emitting vocal sounds again, and I understood as well as before. I had gotten through to her after all, and she was getting through to me in return.

"Where I come from, someone famous can be called a star," said Kitty, "so named because she exists on a higher level than other people, up among the twinkling lights in the night sky."

Famous? What does famous mean?

Kitty thought for a moment. "Known by many people. The more, the better."

Known why? For what reason?

"In my case, *charms*." Kitty gave her head a shake, tossing her mane of dark brown fibers. "My looks are *pleasing... ravishing,* even. My grace and allure doubly so. But my outrageous behavior plays a role, as well."

What do you mean by outrageous? No meaning attached to

the word in my mental translation. It came across as an absolute blank, a hole in a sentence.

"By outrageous, I mean...extreme." Kitty closed one eye, then flicked it open again. "Out of the ordinary. Attention-getting. Scandalous. Something so unusual and excessive, it becomes *legendary*."

Legendary?

"Unforgettable, sir," said Kitty. "People continue to talk about it for ages to come. The person becomes a mythic figure...like *me*, actually." She lifted her garment at the base of her trunk, kicked back one of her lower appendages, and dipped her body while bowing her head. "And *you* were lucky enough to come across me. Now you can say you've met a real, live *legend*."

Lucky. She was right.

I had come in search of stories and songs worth preserving from the end of Ardora; what I'd found was someone who seemed likely to provide all that and more. The things she'd said so far were unlike those related by any inhabitants I'd interviewed, and her appearance so late in Ardora's end-times under such impossible circumstances suggested she had vital information to share.

I had to keep her talking, whatever it took.

Suddenly, though, the plain of roiling nuclear flame shuddered. The thermal updrafts shifted, tossing me around—though Kitty just stood there, unmoving, as if the inferno underfoot were steady as a rock.

"By the way, sir," she said. "What's your name? What shall I call you?"

A word shot out of me before I could stop it. A word

expressed by my fluctuating wavelengths yet feeling strange nonetheless, as if someone else were saying it instead of me.

Paul, I told her. *Call me Paul.*

"SUCH A STRONG NAME." Kitty's mouth curled and widened, exposing the white masticating apparatus within. "I very much approve."

Bobbing on the quickening thermals, I thought for long moments about what I'd said. Probing the depths of my mind, I found no explanation; I could not recall ever being called by the name Paul (or *any* name, for that matter) in my life.

But I also thought going along with it might expedite the interview process…and it seemed to me that time was of the essence.

The raging conflagration of the star's surface bucked and billowed with rising fury. Cyclones of fire whirled around us, lashing out with tongues of blistering emerald plasma. A titanic solar prominence stabbed skyward in the distance, its girth and power more staggering than any solar-borne struc-ture I'd ever seen.

Things were picking up. Ardora was not long for this universe.

The signs were clear to me, as someone who'd barely survived Xynth's untimely demise. Xynth's fire had burned red, not green, at the end, but its apocalyptic progression had otherwise been much the same.

Maybe impending doom wasn't such a bad thing, though.

If the disaster consumed me, perhaps I could make up for not saving my research team on Xynth.

Or maybe it wasn't time for me to die just yet. Maybe I could still save myself if I quickly captured Kitty's stories before they were swept away forever, then launched myself among the stars before the final collapse.

TELL ME MORE ABOUT YOURSELF, Kitty, I said. *Tell me about your outrageous behavior.*

Kitty crinkled her features in a way I didn't understand. As she'd done earlier, she emitted a high-pitched, repetitive vocalization from the tubular linkage between her head and trunk. "Well, people say I once ate a thousand guinea banknote on a bread-and-butter sandwich."

I understood the bare bones of what she was talking about, though I couldn't picture it in the slightest. *And why did you do that?*

"Who says I *did?*"

I thought about it for a moment. *People. You said people say it.*

"People say a *lot* of things, sir." Again, Kitty made the high-pitched sound that I now realized signified amusement. "That doesn't mean they're all true."

The concept of lying was known to me. It came up often in the stories and songs I'd collected. Still, I felt like I was missing something in what she was telling me.

"Here's something else they say I did." Kitty raised a single digit of an upper appendage, perhaps for emphasis. "I fell off a horse in St. James' Park in London, and something happened…something that made me more famous than ever. One of the most famous people in the *world*, in fact."

What was it? I asked.

"What happened that made me more famous, you mean?" she said.

No. I mean what is a horse?

Again, she uttered that sound of amusement. "A great four-legged beast that carries you from place to place…unless it decides to *drop* you."

So what did *happen to make you more famous?*

Kitty looked away, gazing into an especially wild cyclone of fire. "It's certainly a stormy day, isn't it? Makes me wish I'd brought a parasol." Her eyes narrowed, the strips of fine brown hairs above them creasing as her forehead wrinkled. "Though I'm still not quite sure where exactly I was before I got here, to be honest."

London?

Kitty continued to stare at the cyclone and didn't answer.

Ardora shuddered violently, reminding me that time was

growing short. If I wanted to capture Kitty's stories and get them to safety, I had to keep her talking.

You said you fell off a horse in the park. Then what happened?

The upper part of her trunk rose and fell as she inhaled deeply, then let the breath out again. She closed her eyes and shook her head slowly, just once.

Then her eyes shot open, and she swung her head up to gaze in my direction.

"Let's talk about *you* instead." Her mouth curled at the corners again. "Tell me something about yourself, Paul."

Unprepared for the turnabout, I hesitated. *There isn't much to tell.*

"Is this your home, pray tell?" She spread her upper appendages wide to take in the sunscape around us. "Or did you drift in from somewhere else, as I must have done?"

Somewhere else, I told her. *Somewhere far away, where there are many more like me.*

"Many more whats?" asked Kitty. "What *are* you, exactly?"

A person. Just another kind of person.

Kitty's forehead wrinkled, and her eyes narrowed. "I've never met a person who's a glowing silver cloud before, Paul. The people I've known have always looked like me—two arms, two legs, ten fingers, ten toes. Not nearly as *pretty*, mind you, but all the same parts."

The sun rumbled, and another enormous prominence exploded in the distance. Then another.

I tried not to think about all the people who were caught up in the destruction, all the Ardorans going down with the dying star. Their anguish jarred my wavelengths.

I am here on a mission, I told Kitty. *Collecting the stories and music of those who are about to perish in the disaster that is now underway. The end of this great star.*

Her forehead wrinkles deepened. "You're saving *stories*? Why not save the *people* instead?"

They refuse to leave what they love the most. They would rather die than be without it.

"I know the type." Her eyes brightened, and her mouth widened. "I've had admirers like that."

Admirers?

"People who pursued me," she said. "In spite of my apparent lack of interest and the copious rejection I heaped upon them."

Because you were famous?

"Because I was *beautiful*." Kitty reached up and patted the flowing brown tresses draped over her head. "And I still am. *Irresistible*, don't you agree? Even if...even if I'm starting to wonder..." She lowered her appendage, her forehead wrinkling.

Again, the surface of Ardora shook violently.

"I'm starting to wonder if I'm *dead*," said Kitty. "And if this is *Hell* itself."

<hr>

WATCHING another nuclear cyclone spin to life, feeling the fiery surface thrash and explode as multitudes screamed with dread in the distance, I wondered if Kitty might be right. Understanding the bare bones of the word she'd used, I wondered if Ardora might indeed be the Hell she imagined.

"I can't say I don't deserve to be here," she said. "If this is

Hell, that is. I can't deny I've made a lot of mistakes in my life." She cast her gaze downward. "I know I've done my part to make the world a grubbier place. To lower expectations." Kitty drew and released a long breath, then flung up her head with eyes wide and flashing. "But in my defense, the 18th century hasn't exactly been a picnic. As a woman, I've had to fight every step of the way."

But you told me you're a star. You're a legend.

"That doesn't mean I'm a good person, Paul," said Kitty. "Or even an interesting one. All I've done is make up stories and pretend I'm someone special...but the truth is, there has never been anything special about me." She shook her head slowly, forehead furrowed. "I'm just hollow. I'm nothing but surface."

As I watched and listened, I felt sympathetic. I barely knew her, but I felt a connection between us…and a renewed urgency to get what I'd come for, the treasure only she could provide.

There was no way I was going to leave Ardora without at least one of her stories, not if I could help it.

Tell me what happened at St. James' Park, I said. *What happened when you fell off the horse?*

"You're sure you want to know?" She gave me a look I couldn't decipher. "You'll be disappointed."

Yes, I said. *Please tell me.*

KITTY PAUSED, straightened, and fixed her eyes on my wavelengths. She made a noise I hadn't heard before—a loud grunt as if to clear a passage for the words she was about to say.

Then, finally, she spoke.

"When I hit the ground, my skirts flew up," she said. "And everyone saw…that I wasn't wearing any undergarments."

A long moment passed without a word between us, even as the solar storm raged and worsened.

Undergarments?

"See? I *said* you'd be disappointed."

No, it's just that I don't understand why…

"Didn't I *say* I wasn't interesting? What kind of person becomes a *media sensation* for falling off a horse while not wearing any *underclothes?*"

Maybe if you could just explain the significance…

"But hey! Never let it be said I leave an audience unsatisfied! You want a great story?" She folded her upper appendages over her body. "Well, maybe I have one, after all… but it's not about me. It doesn't include a single celebrity, in fact."

Tell me.

"It's about a man," said Kitty. "A man whose family died in a terrible crash that was all his fault. He couldn't face the truth, so he hid away in a hellish hallucination, a nightmare of his own creation."

My wavelengths shifted as I listened. Though it's not quite right to say a radiation field is capable of tensing up, I did compress my cloud in a tighter formation and resonated at a less engaging frequency.

"The end," said Kitty. "Satisfied?"

The end? That was it?

"You want to know what happens next, is that it?" She unfolded her appendages and held them up, shrugging the part of her trunk where they attached. "Well, I'm not much of a storyteller, so why don't *you* tell *me*?"

Tell you what?

"Might this guy snap out of it, do you think?" asked Kitty. "If, say, his imagination were to conjure up someone to intercede? Perhaps an historical figure he has read about, someone with her own set of problems? And by helping her, do you think someone like him might finally find a measure of peace in spite of losing his wife and three children?"

As Kitty's questions washed over me, I wasn't sure what to say next. She seemed to be suggesting that nothing was as it appeared, as if the evidence of my senses and memories was all an illusion.

But for one such as I, a radiation entity grounded in the

physical laws of the universe, the truth of existence is clear. No doubts are possible when the very wavelengths of my being interact continuously with the structure of reality itself.

It is impossible to confuse me about what I know and feel and remember. At least, that was what I thought before Kitty's next words.

"How about if I tell you another story?" she said, giving her fibers a toss. "Maybe you'll like this one better. It's about an actual historical figure—a woman—who ends up sucked through time and space by unknown forces to a place she doesn't recognize..."

Are you talking about yourself? I asked.

Kitty ignored my question. "She's in a place she doesn't recognize, and she is so angry and upset about her wasted life, her so-called *celebrity* that has led to nothing, the emptiness inside her, that she's willing to destroy an entire *universe* to end her misery...and she just might. Because the dying star that she lands on, it turns out, is at the heart of a cosmic chain reaction...and she senses she is linked to it, as if by magic.

"She realizes she has the power to alter the star's pending destruction. She can shift it in such a way that instead of just collapsing into a black hole, it triggers the cosmic reaction... and once that starts, it won't end until the entire universe in which she exists is destroyed."

I hung there, so caught up in what she was saying that I paid little attention to the blistering solar storm raging around us...the end of the sun in progress. Did we have hours or minutes left in the countdown? All I knew for sure was that when the end finally came, anyone not far enough away would be hauled down into the inescapable gravity well of the giant black hole that would form in Ardora's wake.

Kitty gazed at me expectantly. "So how did you like that one, Paul? Was it better than my other story?"

I don't know. I don't...

"Which story do you think is true?" asked Kitty. "Assuming *either* of them is true. The one about the man with the dead family or the one about the woman on the verge of destroying the universe?"

As the fiery upheaval closed in, I considered what she'd said. What if she'd been right the first time, and everything I knew was an illusion designed to hide my own guilt? Or what if her second story was true, and the reality I knew was authentic but teetering on the brink of destruction?

"How do the stories end?" asked Kitty. "If the man wakes from his dream, this universe ends, doesn't it? He gives up on the fantasy and goes back to face the horror of his guilt and loss.

"Or if the woman, in her anger and despair, triggers an interstellar chain reaction with the demise of the sun, the universe ends then, too.

"Either way, all of this ends." Kitty spread her upper appendages and turned in a slow circle, flames licking at her bare feet. "And it ends *soon*, because Ardora is about to die, no matter which story is true.

"So how do you think it should go, Paul?" Kitty stopped turning and raised a hand toward me. "If you had to bet on the outcome, which one would you put your money on? Which grand finale would you pick?

"The end of the universe...or the end of the universe?"

KITTY FELL SILENT, then, as I worked to sort out what she'd told me.

Though a radiation field cannot literally be wrapped up in knots, that was just how I felt at that moment. My first impulse was to flee from the perishing green star without delay. I had what I'd come for—the story of the impossible survivor. Lingering proved nothing, except perhaps that I could be dumb enough to get myself killed because of the mind games of a creature who might not even be real.

Still, I felt compelled to remain a little longer. The sun was ending, trillions were about to plunge into oblivion with it— yet I couldn't quite get myself to leave.

Was it just that Kitty's story of the guilt-ridden man kept nagging at me? That it made me wonder if the truth of my life was very different from what I'd thought it was?

Was it sympathy for tragic Kitty, who lamented her empty life? Did I think, somehow, I could save her—and save the universe in the bargain?

Or was something else holding me there past the point when I should have been gone?

As I hung there, fighting the violent solar winds as they coursed through the apocalyptic melee, I dug deep for the answer. Ardora convulsed, gripped by terrible forces in its core, and I wondered if I had a death wish. Did I feel the need for self-sacrifice because of my failure to save my team from the destruction of Xynth?

Or maybe a death wish had nothing to do with it. Maybe my reluctance to leave was rooted in the *opposite* of a death wish. Perhaps the redemption I sought had more to do with *saving life.*

And maybe the grand finale didn't have to be the end of the universe after all.

Reaching out with my wavelengths, I detected the multitudes of people spanning the fiery orb, all the self-aware flames and flickers and sparks about to be extinguished. I heard their cries of fear and sorrow, loud enough to punch through the howling tempest—a final song, the ultimate expression of their existence.

None of them wanted to leave the home they loved, though none of them wanted to stay and die, either. But why did they have to choose one or the other?

Something Kitty had said earlier rushed back to me. *You're saving stories? Why not save the people instead?*

Good question.

Kitty, I said, moving closer to make myself heard over the deafening pandemonium. *What if there's* another *story?*

She looked at me with forehead creased and eyes narrowed. "Another story?"

What if there's one that neither of us has thought to tell until now? But it turns out to be the best story of all.

AND SO I told her the other story, the one that had come to me, inspired by her...and we agreed it was indeed the best of the lot. We agreed it was the perfect story for the end of the world, the perfect ending to our encounter. Maybe even the whole reason we'd been brought together in the first place.

Then we worked together to make it a reality.

This is what we did: The two of us joined forces to reach out to the people of Ardora. We spoke to all of them at once, linked to trillions of networked minds by my mastery of incorporeal communication. Then, empowered by Kitty's personal magnetism and talent for marketing to the masses, we did together what I could never have accomplished on my own.

We convinced them to leave.

We talked them into pooling their power to break free of Ardora's immense gravity. As attached as they were to their beloved home, this was no easy lift…but we came up with a solution that was accepted by one and all. The solution was to take pieces of Ardora with them, using shrouds of stellar nuclear fire to fuel their journey and comfort them en route. The embers of their home star would keep them company as they plied the great unknown of deep space.

And those embers would enable them to do something else, besides.

Kitty and I saw the proof of it as we soared into space together after the evacuation of Ardora's inhabitants, racing away from the green star as it finally collapsed. Escaping the event horizon of the black hole that was forming in Ardora's place, we gazed out at the darkness of space and witnessed the result of our labors.

A grand new stellar formation spread out before us, a moving constellation composed of the multitude of fire folk and glowing embers that had fled the destruction of Ardora.

As with any starry array, you could see whatever you chose in this formation. It all depended on your personal perspective, connecting the dots to satisfy your own creative impulse and sense of how things should be.

Gazing out at the new constellation, we might have seen the faces of a family who died in a terrible crash, all smiling and mouthing the words, "We love you, Paul! All is forgiven!"

We might also have made out the form of a young Kitty Fisher after falling off a horse, splayed upside-down and underwear-deprived...yet more self-possessed and resolute this time, determined to steer her destiny with quiet dignity and uplift society instead of helping to drag it down.

As for me, I chose to see something entirely different. Something absolutely fitting.

I saw the people of Ardora liberated from their dead home and spreading throughout the galaxy...carrying bits of Ardora like blazing torches into the dark, using them to kindle new stars in the heavens. I saw trillions of them, bringing starry new homes to life from the embers of a cataclysm, choosing to move on by their own terms without letting the grip of the past hold them back.

All of them knowing that stars, like the past, are illusory. Every star looks huge and inescapable when you're close to it —but from a distance, they're all the same, just tiny sparks lighting the way into what might or might not be a brighter tomorrow.

DAVID H. HENDRICKSON

Full-time professional writer David H. Hendrickson has been a writer for many, many years, not only as a fiction writer, but writing thousands of sports articles. He knows writing. And he knows life.

With Dave, you never know what kind of story you will get, which as editor and fan of his work, I love. I find this story especially powerful as a writer myself. Truth and Lies. They are everything, as Dave clearly shows you. Hang on, this story might bite you.

Dave's short fiction has appeared in Best American Mystery Stories, Ellery Queen's Mystery Magazine, Heart's Kiss, *and numerous anthologies, including over a half dozen issues of* Fiction River *and just about every issue of this magazine so far. Check it all out at http://www.hendricksonwriter.com/*

TRUTH AND LIES

DAVID H. HENDRICKSON

I love Lies. She smells of roses. Dozens of red, red roses. Roses with nothing but petals.

No thorns.

She makes a bed of them for me to lie down on. She lies down beside me, holds me to her breasts, and coos sweet nothings into my ear. She strokes my cheek with the softness of a single, delicate fingertip. If she finds a tear there, Lies wipes it away. She wraps her arms around me, and in her embrace I am all I have ever hoped to be.

She tastes like honey. Sweet. Never bitter. Her skin, soft as feathers.

She wears short skirts. High heels. On occasion, fishnet stockings. Bright red lipstick on her soft, moist lips.

It's no secret. She has a tawdry reputation.

But what do I care? I am never happier than when I am with Lies. I wish I never had to leave her.

But when Truth arrives, wearing her starched white shirt,

dark blue tie, and impeccably tailored Armani suit—black with a dark blue pocket square to match the tie—and sternly clicks her black Italian shoes, my beloved Lies must flee. She cannot bear the presence of Truth.

Neither can I.

Truth pretends to be my friend, putting an arm around me, giving my shoulder a squeeze, and smiling. But it's a hard, cold smile, one with no love, joy, or merriment in it. The smile of a sadist. A smile that condemns me to despair, condemns me to my own personal Hell.

"I'm doing this for your own good," Truth says, and grins her almost perfect smile. Perfect except that with its icy coldness it appears ready to crack like a sliver of a glacier cascading into the sea. Perfect except that her bright, white teeth are just a little too sharp. Perfect except that her black eyes stare at you, unblinking, and if you dare return the stare, you are drawn into their darkness as if they have no end.

I don't believe for a minute that Truth has interrupted my time with Lies for my own good. Truth says that she will set me free, but she cares nothing for me or my freedom. She hates Lies, and when she sees the two of us together, so very happy, Truth cannot stand it.

For my own good? Hardly. Truth is a sadist, ever seeking to inflict her pain, upon the likes of me—of everyone!—and upon Lies herself, who she sends scurrying into the shadows, unable to withstand her glare. It's a lust for pain that Truth can never fully satisfy.

And so she persists, each time driving Lies away.

MY OLDEST MEMORY of Truth and Lies was as a short, pudgy little child. Was I four, or five, or six? It does not matter. What matters is that I believed in Lies so fully, so absolutely, and she made me so very, very happy.

She came to me then in the form of Santa Claus. Laugh all you want. Mock me if you will. But I was happy! It was Christmastime and I helped my mother decorate the tree beside the staircase, dressing it with lights and bulbs of all colors and strings of silver tinsel. I squealed with delight when together we climbed the wooden stepladder and she helped me mount the glowing angel atop the tree. For weeks the house smelled of pine and home-cooked cookies: oatmeal and raisin, chocolate chip, and sugar.

I was an only child and thus had my own upstairs bedroom, small and cramped with cheap, second-hand furniture, the wood chipped and discolored with dark blotches sprinkled across its light brown hue. But it was mine. And in that little bedroom, musty with all its little boy smells, I had a dresser against one wall, a desk against the opposite one, and my bed in the middle. And I sat at that desk and wrote my letter to Santa Claus.

Unbeknownst to me, it was really to Lies.

Dear Santa, I printed in awkwardly drawn, scrawling letters. *I have tried very hard to be good.* I went on extolling my virtues that year while explaining the reasons behind my failings, certain that Santa would find merit in the one and understand the other. I then begged that he would bring me the red Schwinn bike I coveted, the one centered on page 235 in that year's Sears catalog. I even included the page number for Santa so there would be no mistake. I watched *Captain*

Kangaroo on TV—never missed a show—and even the Captain agreed that there was no bike like a Schwinn.

I told Santa how I would use my spare baseball cards, the duplicates of bad players—worthless to me despite the intoxicating residual smell of the pink, flat stick of gum that came with each pack and even today takes me back to those cherished days—and I would do like Robby Comeau down the street and attach them to the spokes of the wheels so they would go *thwack, thwack, thwack* as I pedaled proudly down the sidewalk.

And when Christmas morning arrived, I flew down the steps so fast I almost tripped and fell, surely breaking my arm or wrist or neck, but I arrived safely at the landing, and there beside the wonderfully decorated tree was the most poorly disguised gift of all time, red and green wrapping paper around what was undoubtedly the red Schwinn bike from page 235 of the catalog.

I tore that paper off, shrieking with euphoric delight.

"Santa got my letter! Santa got my letter!" I yelled at the top of my lungs, as my parents looked on, my father's arm around my mother, and they shared my joy.

I was happy, so very happy, with what Santa—what *Lies*—had brought me.

It was pure bliss until Truth, in the form of Robby Comeau's older brother, informed me what a fool I was. It was *my parents* who had bought that bike, not Santa Claus.

There was no Santa Claus. No magical appearance from him on the night before Christmas in answer to my carefully constructed letter. Only stupid babies thought that.

A fistful of joy and all of the magic was ripped out of that red Schwinn bike.

By Truth.

Robby Comeau's older brother was right, of course. There was no Santa Claus. And I was just a stupid, little baby, who couldn't help crying at what I'd learned.

But I had been *so* delighted!

Truth hadn't been able to bear my happiness. She'd had to unmask Santa Claus—unmask *Lies*—as a fraud.

For my own good? Because it was time to *grow up*?

Already, I hated Truth.

DON'T BE A BABY, I'm sure you're thinking. It was just Santa Claus. Every kid goes through that.

I don't disagree. I never said I was unique. In fact, I say the opposite. I am everyman. I am everywoman. Only the rarest exceptions walk among us.

We are all told we are special. We are all told we can be anything we want to be. Those are some of the sweetest nothings that Lies whispers in our young, gullible ears. So intoxicating, so hypnotic.

"You're special," we hear, and Lies kisses our forehead and rumples our hair as we hear those words. Words we want to hear. Words we *must* hear, for to think anything different—*"You'll never amount to anything! You're useless!"*—would be intolerable. No, we must hear, "You can be anything!"

When I first heard those words, I decided that I wanted to be an astronaut. I dreamed of floating weightlessly in space... of looking down upon the pale blue globe we call Earth... of walking on the moon, bouncing with every step like Neil Armstrong... of maybe even living on Mars and every night cleaning its dry, red grit from my spacesuit.

I dreamed it all until in the sixth grade nearsightedness forced me to get my first set of glasses, and Truth gleefully told me—I could sense the mocking glee even as the most fraudulent sadness covered her face and heavy-lidded eyes—that astronauts must have perfect twenty-twenty vision. Not a one wore glasses.

And so my dream of becoming an astronaut came crashing down to Earth. I *couldn't* be anything I wanted to be. That lie was exposed.

But I was still special, wasn't I? Surely, that much still had to be true. I was special, but had simply been misguided in my initial choice. No, I wouldn't—couldn't—be an astronaut. I'd instead be a point guard in the NBA. And when I couldn't even make the junior high team, still short and pudgy and strikingly lacking in even the most modest athletic skills, I decided I'd become a leading actor in the movies. And after striking out with the Drama Club—"hopelessly wooden delivery" is the phrase I still recall, I decided, briefly, to become the President of the United States.

No sooner did I decide on a new "anything you want to be" choice than Truth squashed it beneath her Italian-shoed foot like a cockroach on cracked concrete, grinding the sole of the shoe over what remained of that dream long after the initial satisfying crunch.

Eventually, I fell in love with the guitar. At the age of seventeen, still short and pudgy and with a forehead dotted with acne, I fell for a Fender Stratocaster just like the one Eric Clapton used to play "Layla" while with Derek and the Dominos. And for the first time, Truth couldn't slap me down and stomp me underfoot.

I wasn't half bad and I was in love. I'd play that Fender until I got blisters on my fingers and then I kept going. I didn't play that guitar to impress others or to get girls, which was impossible because I was still distinctively unattractive.

I played it because of love. Love of music. Love of the instrument. Love of creating sounds that could maybe, some day, please-God-let-it-happen *move people*.

Soon, only the most highly trained ear could distinguish my "Layla" guitar solo from the master's. Same with "Stairway to Heaven" and "Free Bird." I learned 'em all.

God help me, I was in love.

I believed I was special. And while I might not be able to pursue the most fanciful of goals—astronaut to Mars, point guard in the NBA, the next Dustin Hoffman, or the President of the United States—I believed that now I could be whatever I wanted to be because I had found my true calling. I would be a musician, a guitarist, who would create art people would appreciate, enjoy, and remember.

This was within my reach. I was, after all, special.

And so I spent decade after decade pursuing that dream. Traveling the country. Getting ripped off by one bar owner after another. Getting ignored by one drunk after another. Living hand to mouth. Missing so many meals that I was still short but no longer pudgy. I took on the near emaciated look of the severely addicted, though I never once touched any drug.

I kept going long after every chord of common sense screamed in a cacophonous howl that I was wasting my time.

IN THE END, I wasn't special. Not at all. I was a dime a dozen. If that. Whether performing alone or part of a band. Whether the front man or back in the shadows.

In the approximate words of more than one bar owner after he stiffed me my fair due, "There are a million, billion guys like you. As soon as one of you drops dead, another ten come along to take your place. It don't matter to me. It don't matter to no one."

Believing that I was special, believing that I could be what I so desperately wanted to be—*believing Lies*—I gave my all. In the process, I forfeited all attempts at true love. I even wrote a song about it, "You're Never Home, and I Got Lonely." Not a half bad song and with a catchy guitar riff in the middle, if I may say so myself. But other than a whole lot of drunks in a whole lot of bars, hardly anyone heard it. And seems like no one remembers it at all.

No, don't get me started about true love. Don't you *dare* get me started.

And what did I end up with when it was all said and done?

I'm broke. In every which way. Financially, to be sure. I'll never pay off the hospital bills. But my body is also broken. Hands and fingers now arthritic. The ringing of tinnitus roars in my ears all day like an aural stabbing, the payday for years of turning the volume up to the max.

Nobody remembers me or my music. Whatever joy I gave those who heard me play is forgotten, and perhaps never even existed in the first place.

I wasn't special at all.

Not one bit.

"Only the very select few are special," Truth says to me in a tired tone usually reserved for speaking to simpletons. "That's what makes them special."

Over and over, she says those words, mocking the gullibility of my youth when I believed that I truly was special, and even worse, that same gullibility that continued as an adult.

I'm a fool. At last I know it.

"Acceptance is the first step," Truth says, not fully suppressing a smirk. Then she adds with that duplicitous gleam in her eye, "I'm only trying to help."

———

THE END IS NEAR. I've run the full gamut. I lie in my death bed, gaunt almost to the point of skeletal, my breathing agonized and wheezing, like an accordion being drawn slowly in and out. My ragged clothing is drenched in sweat, both old and new. The sheets reek of urine.

I am, of course, alone. Alone except for Truth.

Would that I be alone.

"You've wasted your life," she says. "You're going down into the ground. Worm food. Ashes to ashes. Dust to dust. Nothing more remains. Your light will be extinguished, and no one will remember."

And then finally, she leaves, whether as one final parting mercy or far more likely, because there's no more sadistic sustenance to suck out of my marrow.

And so I call for Lies to come join me. I plead. I've never needed her more.

Lies, I beg of you, come to me now, I cry out in a deathlike rasp, my mouth and lips dry. Tell me that I was special, even if I was not. Tell me that I will be remembered, even if I have already been forgotten. Tell me that I had worth even if that was no more than a dime a dozen.

I was special! I need to hear it! You can't whisper those words to me when I am young and then fall silent now!

And then I feel her presence all about me. The smell of her roses. The stroke of her feather-soft fingertips upon my cheek. Her kisses upon my ears.

Thank you! From the bottom of my heart, thank you for not abandoning me now.

I love you, Lies. I have always loved you. I have worshipped you all my life.

Lie down beside me now. Forgive the rank smells of death. I can do nothing about them.

Here. Right here. Yes.

Hold me. Forgive me for shaking.

Yes, that is good. Yes.

Now whisper into my ears those sweetest words of all. Tell me that something other than darkness awaits me. It need not be eternal bliss. Perhaps a chance to live it all over again, and next time get it right. Next time, I can be special. Or eternal bliss. That would be best of all. Of course, eternal bliss!

Anything but the darkness.

Yes, I can see the bright light coming for me.

Thank you, my sweet, sweet Lies. Thank you.

It is coming closer now. Closer and closer still.

Bless you for giving me this one last relief. Anything but the darkness.

Lies, I have always loved you. You are the sweetest and fairest of them all.

I will always remember you. Somewhere in your loving heart, Lies, please remember me. Even if you won't, please say that you will.

GOT
STEAMPUNK
MAGIC?
WorldoftheFey.com

ADAM-TROY CASTRO

Adam-Troy Castro's story "Survey" might easily be one of the most disturbing stories ever to appear in these pages. And that is going some for me to say that. So be warned.

Adam is a seasoned professional writer who sold to me and Kris stories in the very first incarnations of the different Pulphouse magazines back in the late 1980s and early 1990s.

This is Adam's fifth appearance in this new incarnation. You can find a lot more information about Adam-Troy's work and his amazing and long career at his web site https://www.adamtroycas tro.com/

SURVEY

ADAM-TROY CASTRO

"**G**OOD AFTERNOON, STEPH. I'M sorry for the delay. I had to finish the outprocessing on one of the prior subjects and it took a little longer than I expected. Would you like a beverage to make you more comfortable? Some water, juice, soda?"

"No, thank you. I'm good."

"The survey can take an hour or more. Are you sure?"

"I'll take a bottle of water, then."

"That's wise. These surveys can be thirsty work, and our guidelines do require our subjects to complete all the questions before receiving their stipend. If you take a break in the middle and return to complete the rest of the questions, you will surrender half of the one thousand dollars. If you take more than one break, or fail to complete the survey, you surrender the payment in its entirety. This is a nonnegotiable provision. Do you understand?"

"Yes."

"You have also been advised that this is, among other things, an exploration of stress on the human animal and that, accordingly, some of the questions may be personal or upsetting?"

"I suppose that's why you're paying so much."

"Yes. Have you participated in many of these studies during your time on campus?"

"One or two."

"Tell me about one of them."

"It was for the Psych Department. They asked me to watch some old Western on DVD. Bend of the River, starring James Stewart. Afterward, they asked me to take a quiz about the plot, to see how much I retained."

"I'm surprised that a young woman your age even knows who James Stewart was."

"I didn't. Not him or the other guy, Rock Hudson. I think that was probably the first Western I ever saw."

"Was it good?"

"It was okay, I guess. I don't really like old movies."

"You remembered the title and the name of the star."

"I have a good memory."

"And you were paid for this?"

"That's why I did it. They were paying fifty dollars."

"Not much work for a quick fifty."

"No."

"And you even got to see a movie."

"Well, not one I liked much, but still."

"It doesn't seem like that study would have had much of a practical application."

"I wouldn't know. They never did tell me what they hoped to learn."

"I suppose not. We plan to be a little more forthcoming, when we're done. And as you know, we're offering substantially more than fifty dollars, with a chance of payment on an entirely different order of magnitude if you elect to continue with further stages of the study. This is a long-term project that's been running for over thirty years, and we have had more than one student in your financial circumstances stay with us for the entire course of their university educations, some earning so much that they graduated free of debt."

"You're kidding. It can be that much?"

"This study is underwritten by one of the largest fortunes in the United States, with significant contribution from the American taxpayer. I assure you that it can be that much, and that if you do well, it can lead to lucrative employment opportunities upon graduation. But first you have to get through the initial survey."

"I'll get through it. I can use the money!"

"Yes, which is why we circulated the flier among the work-study population. Ah, here's your water. Nice and cold. It's been on ice. Thank you, Jane. Will there be anything else, Steph? Once again, would you like to use the restroom before we begin?"

"No, I'm okay."

"Do you understand that this session will be monitored?"

"Yes."

"Do you also understand that the recording will enter the permanent archives of this project?"

"Yes."

"Do you understand that you are attached to leads measuring your heart rate, your respiration, your blood pressure, and multiple other metabolic indicators, and that this information will be used in this study?"

"Yes."

"Are you all right with that?"

"Sure."

"Please sign here, acknowledging your understanding of these terms."

"There you go."

"All right, then. Let's start the recorder. Survey code 2793MB, subject Stephanie Halpern, preferred name Steph. Age: nineteen. Sophomore, Communication Arts. Steph, will you please say something innocuous, to calibrate your voice level?"

"Umm. Hi. How do I sound?"

"Just fine. Now something with lots of Ps, to make sure we get no mike pops."

"Peter Piper picked a peck of pickled peppers."

"Most people say that. Did you get that, everybody? Ah, it looks like we have a green light and are ready to go."

"Great."

"Steph, do you assert for the record that you have agreed to participate in this survey of your own free will? Say, 'Yes, I do,' if so."

"Yes, I do."

"Do you understand that no payment will be tendered until you answer the final question?"

"Yes, I do."

"Do you also acknowledge agreement that some of these questions may be of a personal or upsetting nature?"

"Yes, I do."

"Steph, the man now entering the room works for our security division. His presence is one of the requirements of this survey. He will not be interfering with us in any way, unless there's trouble."

"What kind of trouble could there be?"

"As we have noted, some of these questions can be upsetting. One or two of your predecessors in this study have succumbed to stress responses and physically assaulted their interlocutors. I do not personally believe that I have anything to fear from you, but the project leaders now require the presence of armed security, to forestall such eventualities. Rest assured that if this does become necessary, he is instructed to restrain you with minimal force. You will, however, sacrifice the promised stipend. Do you acknowledge understanding of the reason for his presence?"

"I'm not sure I like this."

"You can leave, or you can acknowledge understanding of the reason for his presence."

"Umm. Okay. I acknowledge understanding of the reason for his presence."

"Steph, what is your life's greatest ambition?"

"Umm. You mean professionally?"

"That would be a fine place to start."

"I want to work in television."

"Creative or corporate?"

"Creative."

"You want to write? To tell stories?"

"I'm no writer. I just want to be involved in production somewhere."

"Any specific ideas?"

I'm still figuring that out."

"Excellent. Is it fair to say that your ambitions are at least partially driven by wanting to make a difference in the world?"

"…That almost sounds like you're mocking me. But yes."

"I'm not mocking you. It's perfectly normal for someone your age to still be exploring her options, to still be forming plans for the future. But this will help us, moving forward."

"Okay."

"Steph, are you a violent person?"

"No."

"Has anybody ever accused you of being a violent person?"

"No."

"Excluding childhood incidents prior to, let us say, age twelve, have you ever struck another human being?"

"Yes."

"How many incidents?"

"Two or three, I guess."

"Describe one."

"A couple of years ago, I went out with a guy who got upset when I told him I wasn't going to sleep with him. I had to slap him to let him know I was serious."

"Did he desist?"

"Yes."

"You were lucky. Any incidents more serious than that?"

"No."

"Did you ever draw blood?"

"No."

"You never had cause to scratch the face of anyone as pushy as that boy?"

"No."

"Forgive me: Is this because no other boys showed you equivalent disrespect, or because you were never again that recalcitrant?"

"That's a disgusting question."

"Do you refuse to answer it?"

"No. There were other guys I had to say no to, and other guys I said yes to, but nobody else I ever had to fight to get them to listen."

"All right, then. We won't ask for the percentages. Are you seeing someone now?"

"Yes."

"Have you ever been angry with him?"

"Yes."

"Did you argue?"

"Yes."

"Was there any name-calling?"

"I called him an asshole."

"Do you still believe him to be asshole?"

"He was definitely being an asshole that day!"

"I don't need to know the details. On a scale of one to ten, with one being absolute calm and ten being totally out-of-control, shrieking rage, how close did you come to slapping him then?"

"I guess a...four?"

"Four. Excellent. Steph, is it accurate to say that you have never been part of any military force?"

"Oh, no."

"You mean, no, you have been, or no, you haven't been?"

"I'm sorry. I mean, no, I haven't been."

"Is it therefore accurate to say that you've never had to use lethal force against another human being?"

"Yes. That's accurate."

"Steph, do you consider yourself a pacifist?"

"No."

"Is it accurate to say that you have never done harm of any permanent nature to any human being?"

"Yes."

"What about to animals?"

"What? No, of course not!"

"Do you eat meat?"

"Yes."

"So you do harm to animals, but not actively."

"Yes."

"If you were placed in some extreme survival situation

where you had to hunt and butcher some animal or starve, do you think you could do what was necessary?"

"I used to go fishing with my Dad. Does that count?"

"I will take that as a yes. Steph, do you consider yourself a liberal, a conservative, a moderate, or someone who isn't interested in politics?"

"A moderate."

"Do you consider yourself a good person?"

"I try to be."

"An idealist?"

"If that means, do I have ideals, sure."

"Excellent. Now, this is where the questions get a little more complicated."

"All right. Should I be scared?"

"That's up to you. Do you want to continue?"

"I'm okay so far."

"For the next part, you will need your pencil."

"Okay."

"I'm now handing you a graphic on a sheet of paper. Please describe the illustration."

"Three people."

"Can you characterize the drawing, for the record?"

"Characterize it? You mean, describe it?"

"Yes."

"Okay. It's not a realistic drawing, not one that tells me much. It's just three identical black outlines, vaguely shaped like people."

"In short, Steph, is it the kind of drawing you would produce if you had three human beings lie flat on the ground and outlined them with chalk or masking tape?"

"Like they do in murder investigations, right?"

"Yes. Except that we intend these outlines to represent upright, living figures."

"Yes. I can see that."

"Can you tell anything about the individuals illustrated here? Their ages? Their genders? Their racial background? Their politics? Their clothing?"

"No."

"Is it fair to say that they could be anybody?"

"They seem to be adults."

"That's excellent. Children have different bodily proportions. So do some adults, of course — the height-challenged, the deformed, the obese, the disabled, amputees, and so on. I will, however, establish of these outlines that they could very well represent adults of any of these outlying physical constituencies. For the sake of the next exercise, you need only imagine three people living somewhere in the world, their names and circumstances unknown to you. Each one of them could be anybody, from some Mumbai street person to whatever famous musician whose work you enjoy most."

"Okay."

"Is it fair to say that you have no opinion on any of these people? Positive or negative?"

"Yes."

"You are wholly impartial?"

"I can't wait to see where you're going with this."

"Please answer the question. You are wholly impartial?"

"Yes."

"Okay. Now you will play God, for a moment. You will use your pencil to draw a big X over one of these three outlines, in effect killing one of these three unknown individuals. Use whatever imaginary criterion you have. Decide that he's a Nazi war criminal or just an asshole like that boy you once had to slap. Kill him by drawing an X."

"Okay."

"I can see which figure you crossed out, but for the audio record, was it the outline on the left, the outline on the right, or the one in the middle?"

"For the record, it was the one on the right."

"You decided that this individual did not deserve to live and, as a result, some assassin staking out that individual just walked up to them, wherever they are in the world, and put a bullet in their brain."

"Yup."

"Did you feel any sense of satisfaction on killing this person?"

"No."

"Do you feel any guilt?"

"It's just an outline on a sheet of paper."

"Yes, Steph, it is. But this is the point in our session where I advise you that this exercise has never been hypothetical."

"What?"

"I never told you that the three people represented by these figures were imaginary. I told you that they were upright, living people, somewhere in the world. One minute ago, all three of them were living human beings, minding their own daily business. All three of them were under surveillance by representatives of this study, and all three of them were targeted for a bullet in the brain, on your say-so.

You elected which one was going to die. Do you see the light that just went green on my console?"

"...Yes."

"That light confirms that the individual you selected is already dead."

"That's not funny."

"It is not meant to be."

"I get this. This is like, I read about it last semester, what's it called...the Milgram Experiment. They coerced people into giving others electric shocks. Except that the buttons they were pressing weren't hooked up to anything. This is like that."

"I'm impressed that you can cite the Milgram Experiment. You're a smart young lady. But this is the precise opposite of the Milgram Experiment. In that case, participants were encouraged to believe that they were doing real harm, when they were not. Here, you were given every reason to assume that your kill order was not real, when your decision actually did represent life-or-death consequences. Rest assured, Steph. You just ordered the death of an actual human being."

"Stop saying that!"

"Please observe the monitor."

"Oh, my God."

"This is a street scene in Yangon, also known as Rangoon, in Myanmar. That unfortunate woman you see bleeding out is one Daw Kham Keow, age thirty-four. You can tell from the damage to her cranium that the firearm used in her execution was powerful enough to ensure her immediate death. You can also tell that our assassin is nowhere in sight. It may interest you to know that your chosen target was a mother and the sole supporter of her four children, all of whom will now become wards of the — "

"Turn it off!"

"As you wish. If you're interested, the two other people you could have chosen to eliminate were one Marlie DeBauer, eighty-seven, a resident of a retirement community in Boca Raton, Florida; and Ga-Heon Teitikai, twenty-four, a resident of Tarawa in the island nation of Kiribati."

"This is bullshit!"

"If you are having any difficulty processing this information, reflect that with the same act you also saved the lives of Marlie and Ga-Heon, both of whom are still breathing only because you directed the fire somewhere else. It can be said that all three were endangered, and that you selflessly saved two of them."

"I'm leaving!"

"That is your right. However, our security officer here has been instructed to keep you in this room until you have been told why you may not want to."

"Fuck you!"

"The two individuals whose lives you spared are hostages to your continued participation. I can promise you that if you terminate the survey at this juncture, the protection you have provided them will be rescinded, and they will also be cooling sacks of meat by the time you make it to the hallway. You will, in case you're wondering, be sent all the relevant photographs and local news coverage, to confirm that this is not hypothetical."

"You son of a bitch! You sick, sadistic — "

"By all means: Get it out."

" — piece of shit — "

"Most people taking this survey respond as you have, at about this point in the process. Some succumb to total hysteria and are unable to continue, regardless of the consequences. It has been our experience that the most principled, the most principled, do regain control of themselves and push on, recognizing that they have no other choice. I advise you to drink some of your water now. It is what it appears to be and is not adulterated with any mood-altering substances. Taking a pause of that nature will help clear your mind for the next phase."

"What makes you think y-you can — "

"The answer to that question is 'experience.' As I told you at the outset, this project has been ongoing for thirty years. It has included thousands of people and involved substantial investments in infrastructure, up to the very highest corridors of power. I believe I can get away with this because everybody involved in this project always has, and it would take a rebellion far beyond your powers or mine to stop it. Now take a drink of water."

"Oh, God."

"Do what I say. It's just water. No unadvertised substances to affect your reactions."

"I don't believe you."

"I have not lied to you yet. Hydrate. Get your breathing under control."

"You son of a bitch."

"Good girl. Listen to me. We know that this has been traumatic. It's possible that, later on, after you leave this facility, you might want to indulge in something alcoholic. In that event, you may use some of your stipend to go on a total bender, as approximately twenty-seven percent of our participants do. It's wholly understandable. Or you may wish to go even harder. If you end up feeling that the rest of your life now offers no options beyond seeking total oblivion, or destroying yourself, then we have ample supplies of crack and meth and a staff of medical experts fully trained to instruct you in the techniques required to surrender the rest of your life to their habitual use. Our people can, if you wish, take you through one safe dose and let you go, or, as some past participants have requested, guide you all the way down to the comforts of rock bottom in one of the facilities we maintain for that purpose. But right now, water will do."

"F-fuck you!"

"You need to internalize this, Steph: I have heard that many times, from any number of clean-cut young men and sweet young women before you. It will do you no good to keep on saying that, because it affects me not at all and does not change your predicament in the slightest. In the meantime, we must either move on to the next phase, or sacrifice the two innocents whose lives you have saved. Should I give the kill orders?"

"No! Don't! I'll cooperate!"

"Marlie and Ga-Heon are accordingly out of danger. See how simple that is? Now we move on to the next part of the survey. For the record, I am now handing you another sheet of paper, bearing graphic representations of five more individuals. Do you acknowledge receipt?"

"Oh, God."

"Failing to answer the question a second time will have the same effect as drawing an X over all the outlines. Do you acknowledge receipt?"

"I...acknowledge receipt, fucker."

"Will you please tell me the difference between these five humanoid outlines and the three you were provided before?"

"These...look like..."

"Trailing off does no good. Please finish the sentence."

"Ch-children."

"That is correct, Steph. In point of fact, these five outlines represent five existing individuals between ages four and fourteen. They may be of any nationality, any race, any gender, any religious background. To make things more interesting, I will tell you that one is an impoverished orphan living in a refugee camp who can hear the pounding drumbeat of war every night from the pallet she shares with four others. Another is the unsuspecting child of a billionaire who believes that the paid companions with whom he shares today's expensive play are friends, and not operatives fully prepared to deliver him to the fate you might select. The three others are individuals of more middling circumstances, though of course of diverse backgrounds; all in all, a handful of lives that would never intersect in any other way, except in this moment when all five sit represented on the sheet before you."

"And I have to d-decide which one's going to die?"

"No. We don't expect you to decree death for a child. Too many test subjects have fallen into complete paralysis at the very prospect."

"…What, then?"

"You are to select two. One of those two will be blinded with acid, but will otherwise enjoy whatever opportunities are presented by life circumstances. Who knows, it might even be the billionaire's son, who's never going to want for anything, anyway. The other will be taken from home and delivered to a dark, airless room at a black site known to us, there to live as long as medical science can ensure his or her health, but never again allowed the company of another human being, rather to be doomed to an existence where the key question — Why? — will never be answered."

"Oh, God."

"If you select neither, or if you refuse, then all five will be abducted and delivered to sex traffickers. We have a particular dealer in mind. I could provide you with the details of the treatment they will receive under his stewardship, but you don't need to put yourself through that. You just need to know that if you mark two figures with the X, the remaining three will avoid that fate entirely, and that one of your selected two will only suffer a disability with which many millions of people are able to function every single day. The path of lesser evil seems obvious, but again, a certain percentage of subjects who passed this way before you were unable to force themselves to make the selection, and so they chose hell for all five by default."

"I can't do it!"

"That is, as established, a possible outcome. In such a case, you will know for the rest of your life that what happened to all five was your fault. And we will make sure that, wherever you live, however far you attempt to run, you will receive regular photographic updates of how they're faring."

"I'll kill myself first!"

"This will be among your options. Again, once we are done, if that is your desire, we will be happy to provide you with expert assistance as to methods and procedures. But it won't affect what happens to these five. Your only means of saving three (four, really, because blindness is not all that bad compared to the greater threat that's been made) is to provide your marks."

"I f-fucking swear to God, I will k-kill you with my bare hands, someday."

"A genuine possibility, Steph, but one outside the scope of this survey, and one that won't affect this particular decision. You are running out of time. I think I should start the clock. You have thirty seconds to save three by condemning two. Starting now."

"No, wait!"

"Twenty-five. Twenty."

"Why are you doing this?"

"Almost down to ten. Now. Nine. Eight."

"FUCK YOU!"

"The subject is overwrought right now, but for the record,

she has drawn the two X's that were required, one on the figure furthest to the left and one on the figure in the center. Her decisions are made. She is two-thirds of the way through the survey and has only one section left to complete."

"...No more. Please."

"I see from the green light on my console that one child has been blinded, and...yes — that the other has now been taken into custody and is being delivered to her new life. Would you like to see the video evidence?"

"...no..."

"I promise you, Steph, this next part will the last bit, for today. And because it is the most difficult choice of the bunch, you will be provided with the greatest amount of prior intelligence."

"I don't want to."

"Catatonia is one of your options, Steph. We understand that you might want it and we do have medical means of inducing it. But you might prefer the others I am empowered to offer."

"Please, just let me go. I won't tell anybody."

"Of course you won't. We can dispatch operatives to surveil and, if necessary, eliminate people from all walks of life, all over the globe; you think we can't prevent you from trying to do something about what you know? Please. If it even occurs to you to open your mouth, we'll know it. But you won't. Most people who get as far as you have may suffer emotional problems and suicidal ideation, but they do know the difference between what's feasible and what's not, and don't make matters worse with futile gestures like going to newspapers that nobody reads anyway. They understand that going to the authorities is ridiculous, because we are the authorities — especially if they stick around to ask questions, because they are then told everything they need to know. Let me ask you another version of the same question I posed before. What do you want out of life? Money? Power? Influence? The chance to make a difference? You might qualify for all of that."

"I j-just want to go home."

"You're almost there. You just have this last bit left, and once it's done, you can either return to your life with a thousand dollars in your pocket, or you can join us and be drawn into decisions of even greater import: who lives, who dies, who succeeds, who fails, which economies rise and which ones fall, which injustices are righted and which are allowed to fester until they burst open, laying waste to entire regions with the heat of all that incubated corruption. By the time you're thirty, you can be one of the people pulling the strings behind the scenes, someone richer than you ever dreamed of being, and I can promise that you will no longer feel what you feel now, not anymore. You can — "

"Eat me, you sadistic piece of shit, I just want it over!"

"Do you acknowledge receipt of this last sheet of paper?"

"Yes."

"Please describe for the record what you see there."

"Circles. One, two, three…ten circles."

"Steph, those ten circles represent regional populations. Cities, countries. In some cases, hundreds of lives, in others, thousands or even tens of thousands of lives; places that represent entirely different cultures, creeds, and societies. They are residents of democracies, of dictatorships and theocracies, of places prosperous or damned by poverty. Nine of them will continue to bump along the way they have in recent times. The tenth will — ”

“I pick one?”

“Yes, and that one will — ”

“I’ve drawn my X.”

“I can see that. Do you want to know what’s going to happen there?”

“Won’t it make the news?”

“Of course. So will a lot of other catastrophic events. Without specific knowledge, you will never know which one was precipitated by your own X.”

“Then I don’t want to know. I don’t want to hear a goddamned thing.”

“For the record, then, you’ve declined all post-verdict follow-up on the specifics of a decision that will negatively affect an entire regional population, out of acknowledgment that there is no way that dwelling on this intelligence could do you any good. Is that an accurate way to summarize your reasoning?”

“Yes, damn it. Yes!”

“That’s a wise coping mechanism.”

“I don’t care what you think.”

“No, honestly, Steph — that’s precisely the reaction we wish to see by this point in the process. It’s been a very successful session.”

“Do I get to leave now?”

“With this understanding: that there will be a mandatory exit interview in forty-eight hours. If you have not committed suicide by then, you will be required to return. At that point, we will tell you the results of our evaluation and you will tell us whether your decision-making ability qualifies you for further sessions with this organization, with more decisions of increasing levels of consequence, for accordingly greater levels of remuneration. Before you go, I should mention that as an unadvertised result of this session, you will no longer have to complete course work in any of your classes this semester; we understand that the trauma suffered by many of our subjects does impact academic performance and can therefore guarantee full credit for all classes on your current schedule, at a 4.0 grade point average. If you do decide to continue your association with us — "

"Oh, fuck off. I get it. I get it. I've had all I can take of your goddamned face today."

"What are you going to do?"

"I don't know."

"I can tell you that my superiors will be pleased with how you took control of the last part of the survey. They appreciate that kind of decisiveness."

"They can get fucked, too."

"I feel confident that the opportunities available to you will be significant."

"I don't want to hear that right now."

"Should I arrange the appointment for your follow-up interview?"

"I may jump off a bridge on the way home. I don't even want to live right now."

"Will you promise to wait two days? Hear what's being offered? Learn what other kinds of vital decisions need to be made? What sort of life you can have?"

"That's what's supposed to happen? I'm supposed to will-ingly give up what remains of my soul now, to join you evil shits?"

"Well, first you have to pick up your thousand dollars on the way out. You earned it."

"Fuck you."

"Two days, Steph."

"Two days."

"Yes."

"To find out what other kind of relentless monster I get to be."

"To be offered further involvement in this project, yes."

"Fuck you."

"And to qualify for substantial employment opportunities upon graduation. Will we be seeing you then?"

"Oh, God. I don't want to be this person. Please don't let me spend my life being this person."

"Steph?"

"Please."

"Steph. We do need to make this appointment."

"...What time?"

O'NEIL DE NOUX

O'Neil De Noux takes his amazing skills as one of the best writers of detective fiction working today and gives us another story in the colorful and clearly unique world of New Orleans with Detective John Raven Beau. The places and events and characters just come alive in O'Neil's powerful stories.

O'Neil has published about fifty novels with more coming regularly. His awards include The United Kingdom Short Story Prize, the Shamus Award (for best private eye fiction), the Derringer Award (for excellence in mystery short fiction) and Police Book of the Year.

Two of his stories have appeared in the prestigious Best American Mystery Stories *annual anthology and I noticed he had another in the recommended reading for this last year's volume. He won the Shamus for a story in 2020. You can find out a lot more about his work at his website <u>http://www.oneildenoux.com/</u>*

A GATHERING AT LAKE ST. CATHERINE

O'NEIL DE NOUX

When he reached the top of the levee, Detective John Raven Beau put on his extra-dark Ray Ban sunglasses and surveyed the scene – a burned out camp next to the brown water of Lake St. Catherine, brown pelicans gliding in line over this salt-water, south Louisiana lake at the eastern edge of Orleans Parish, which made the levee he stood on within the city limits of New Orleans.

Behind Beau, his unmarked police car sat parked along the shoulder of Highway 90, next to the appropriate mile marker, his blue suit coat folded across the front seat. Beau shoved his portable police radio into the back pocket of his pants and loosened his light blue tie on his way down the levee, toward the camp where the victim's daughter said she'd meet him. With no other car parked on Highway 90, Beau figured she was late. She was too anxious on the phone to be a no-show.

It was hotter closer to the water, but Beau expected that.

Perspiration began working its way down his temples, dampening his freshly-cut dark brown hair. The steamy air, washed in by a lake breeze, smelled of salt and was laced with the scent of burned wood. The camp, suspended on creosote pilings at the water's edge, was still waterlogged from the fire boat water used to put out the fire.

Beau heard a voice and instinctively moved his hand to his stainless-steel nine millimeter Beretta in its canvas holster on his right hip. He spotted her a moment later, behind the camp, next to the water. Standing on what was left of a boat dock, she was feeding popcorn to ducks, mallards mostly, green headed males and brown females.

He pulled his hand away from his weapon and took off his sunglasses.

She wore a sleeveless green blouse and tan slacks, her black hair cropped short. She turned as he approached and stood, staring with wide brown eyes. She was tall, only a few inches shorter than Beau's six-two frame. He tried not to react to her beauty, to her classic African features, silk-chocolate skin and thick, sensuous lips painted a deep red.

"I'm Detective Beau."

"Catherine Oubre," she said as she reached out her right hand, which Beau shook. She held his hand an extra moment, her dark eyes staring into Beau's light brown eyes.

"You're only part Cajun, aren't you?" she said. "Like me."

Beau nodded. "My mother's Oglala Sioux."

"My mother was African-American." A slight smile came to her lips. "Don't know which tribe."

She let go of his hand and nodded to the camp. "My daddy

lived here fifty-one years. I lived here for twenty." She couldn't be much older than that.

Beau, who just turned twenty-nine, put his glasses back on and looked at the burned hulk where they'd found the charged body of sixty-eight year old Eldrich Oubre two days earlier. When the autopsy surfaced a .22 pellet in Oubre's cranium, Homicide was called in and Beau assigned the case.

"It was arson," Beau said. "Arson investigators found accelerant residue. Gasoline."

She nodded. "I spoke with them this morning. They said you were in charge of the case now."

Beau nodded. Homicide outranked arson.

Catherine turned toward the lake and folded her arms. "For the last two years the oil people have been trying to push my daddy off his land." She pointed to a large cypress tree next to the burned camp. "My daddy planted that tree forty years ago."

Shielding her eyes with a hand, she looked at Beau and continued.

"My parents claimed this land under Louisiana's adverse possession law. Ever hear of that law?"

Beau nodded again. "If someone lives continually and publicly on land for thirty years, they own the land. Regardless of who has title to the land."

Catherine seemed surprised that he knew that particular law, which wasn't part of the criminal code.

"Two years ago, right after my mom died, my daddy got an eviction notice from Pelikan Oil Company. We've been fighting them ever since." Catherine stepped back up on the dock. "My daddy killed a twelve-foot gator under here once. It was eating his ducks." She spread her arms. "These are my daddy's ducks."

Catherine Oubre spent the next five minutes explaining how she was an only child, like Beau, and how her father lived off the land, like Beau's father had. Eldrich Oubre fished and hunted rabbits, squirrels and nutria, caught little green turtles.

"We got fifteen cents apiece for the turtles. We raised vegetables and grew those orange trees." Catherine pointed to a stand of small trees lining the bottom of the levee.

Leaning back against the dock she went on to explain how they collected Spanish moss used for stuffing car seats and mattresses and life preservers at a penny-and-a-half a pound.

She focused those dark brown eyes at Beau and said, "We were poor. Dirt poor, as the saying goes. Have you ever been poor, Detective Beau?"

Beau felt a lump in his throat as memories of his childhood flashed in his mind, of fishing the dark brown water of Vermilion Bay with his father, hunting coons and nutria and swamp rabbits in the deep swamp of Southwestern Louisiana, of living in the old Cajun daubed house his grandfather built by hand, its walls packed with swamp mud to keep out the weather, of going hungry some nights and feasting when the hunting was good. Beau could almost see his father's craggy face smiling at him, like the time Beau landed a fat, twelve pound yellow catfish on Bayou Brunet.

"Was that a nod?" Catherine asked.

"Yep." Beau took in a deep breath. "I grew up poor, on water just like this. Vermilion Bay. Didn't even know I was poor 'till I went to school. The other kids let me know right away."

"Me too." Her voice was a whisper.

Beau walked up the partially burned steps of the camp, stopping before reaching the top and looked at the charred remains of a sofa, refrigerator, table, chairs.

"You going all the way in?" Catherine called out from below.

Beau shook his head. "I've seen the crime scene photos." He came back down, noting the scorched generator next to the camp. He pulled the small notepad from his rear pocket and clicking his ball point pen. "Anyone else live around here?"

Catherine pointed down the levee to a distant camp. "That's Mr. Jeansonne's. Like everyone around here, he fishes and hunts. He was my daddy's friend." Turning around, Catherine pointed in the opposite direction. "Mr. Nunez lives about a mile that way. He has a shrimp boat."

"Know anyone who'd want to hurt your father?" Some obvious questions had to be asked.

"Only the oil company."

"Anyone in particular there?"

"A Mr. Regent sent some threatening letters. Threatening to physically remove Daddy from his land."

When Beau asked where the letters were, Catherine nodded to the burned camp.

"Did your father own a twenty-two?"

Catherine shook her head. "He had a four-ten shotgun."

Beau remembered seeing what was left of the shotgun in one of the pictures of the burned camp. Beau slipped his pad and pen away.

"Let's go see this Jeansonne."

They walked on the grass at the base of the levee, the sun hot on their heads, the scents of lake mud and salt water thick in the humid air, scents more familiar to Beau than the magnolias and roses of New Orleans' Garden District.

The only sound came in the squawks from a small flock of seagulls diving to the water and rising again. Sandpipers raced along the tiny sand beach at the water's edge, stopping to pluck the occasional insect.

Jeansonne's camp was also on pilings, a screen porch surrounding the unpainted wooden camp. The screen was patched in places, giving it the look of an old quilt. There was an aluminum, flat bottom boat moored against the tiny dock.

"Monsieur Jeansonne!" Catherine called out.

"Come on up dere," a voice with a thick Cajun accent called back.

Beau led the way up to the porch where a dark-complected man with long salt-and-pepper hair sat on an old wooden rocking chair. He wore a gray tee-shirt and baggy jeans and smoked a pipe. He was barefoot.

Catherine introduced them and Beau saw the man glance at the gold, star-and-crescent badge clipped to the front of Beau's belt. Jeansonne asked them to sit and they sat on wooden folding chairs.

"It was a shock," Jeansonne said. "Me and Eldrich been here so long, I don' know wha' to do."

"Where were you here when it happened?"

Jeansonne pointed to the lake. "I fished all night. Lef' to fish before de sun set and come home in de middle of de dey. De fire boat was still dere with de hoses and de water and Eldrich place was ... smokin'."

"Did you see Eldrich before you left that day?"

"Mais no."

"Did you see anyone around his place?

"Mais no. De' last time I seen Eldrich was de' day before dat'. He was on his dock and I go wif' my boat and we wave. He was feedin' de' duck."

"Did you see any boats in the area that day?"

"Jus de' Pelikan Oil crew boat. Dey sniff around for de' oil, I guess."

Beau asked if Jeansonne had any trouble with Pelikan Oil. Jeansonne said he hadn't since he'd only lived there ten years he had to leave. Apparently his camp had been abandoned by the previous occupant and Jeansonne didn't own it or build it, like Eldrich Oubre.

"Did you get any letters from Pelikan?"

"Jus' one. It say I gotta go. I trew' it away. Dey' come get me off one day and I guess I go."

Jeansonne had known Eldrich Oubre for ten years, but they weren't close. Not talking for months at a time. "We all keep to ourself' down here."

Beau asked about Nunez and Jeansonne huffed, claiming he had little to do with Nunez. Nobody did. "Nunez is what you call a hermit. He don' like no body."

"Do you own a twenty-two?"

"Mais no. Got a 20 gauge shotgun. Eldrich got a shotgun, too."

"Nunez have a gun?"

"Me, I don' know."

After getting the man's full name, date of birth and social security number – Jeansonne had to dig a dog-eared card from his cigar box of papers – Beau left his card in case the man thought of anything else.

"I got no phone," Jeansonne said.

Beau pulled two quarters and two dimes from his pocket and smiled slyly as he suggested the old man find a pay phone.

"I know dey got dem tings." Jeansonne was ribbing him now. "I seen dem."

Beau and Catherine crossed the levee and took his car to the next mile post. Nunez lived in a slightly larger camp, also suspended on creosote pilings. No one was home and no boat around, either. Catherine seemed relieved.

"You got Mr. Jeansonne's name and all to check him through the police computer, didn't you?" She said.

"You never know. He could be a mass murderer."

On their way back to the car, Beau asked, "How'd you get out here today?"

"I took the bus."

"Come on. I'll drive you back in." Beau lead the way up the grassy levee. "How about some lunch?"

"I'm not hungry."

Reaching the top of the levee, Beau turned and looked into those dark brown eyes. "You have anything else to do? Have lunch with me."

Catherine nodded slowly, turned and looked back at the lake, shielding her eyes once again with both hands. She took in a deep breath, then followed Beau down the levee to his police car.

"I have an ulterior motive," he said as he opened the front passenger door of his black Chevy Caprice. Catherine's eyes narrowed. He smiled. "You've got to know a good place to eat around here."

She did. Tauzin's Eat-N-Gas had been a busy truck-stop along Highway 90, before Interstate-10 was built. It still served some of the best seafood, and sold gasoline to locals, but the big rigs were gone. Beau and Catherine had soft-shell crabs and drank Barq's, the root beer with bite, rather than a cold beer, which Beau would have preferred, if he didn't have a lot of work to do on this case.

Not wanting to disturb her meal, Beau waited until they drove away to ask about Nunez. She shrugged and said he wasn't a very nice man. She saw him kill a stray dog once and thought he probably ate it.

"He's a real hermit," she concluded. Her father seemed had no problem with Nunez, however. Eldrich got along with everyone.

Beau didn't say it. At least one person didn't get along with Eldrich.

Catherine Oubre lived in the single student's dorm at the University of New Orleans, which she attended on full academic scholarship. Beau managed to learn she was majoring in Marine Biology and worked part time at The Copy Center on Leon Simon Boulevard.

As Beau turned into the university campus, he saw tears welling in Catherine's eyes. He parked, walked around and opened her door for her. She climbed out and he asked if she was going to be all right.

She nodded, not looking at him at all and said. "I wanted my daddy to see me graduate more than anything."

Closing the door, Beau watched her move away and knew, no matter how long it took, he'd catch Eldrich Oubre's killer.

"That's a fact, Jack," he said aloud to himself.

He could still smell her light perfume in the car when he climbed back in, like a reminder. Like a reminder.

———

Before going to Mr. Regent's office, Beau did a little background check and learned the man was Jefferson D. Regent, IV, with an exclusive uptown address on Audubon Boulevard. A graduate of Tulane Law School, Regent was admitted to the bar before becoming an oil company executive.

Two hours after dropping Catherine Oubre at her dorm, Beau walked into the outer office of Pelikan's Director of Operations on the fortieth floor of the glass-and-chrome

Louisiana Entergy Center on Poydras Street, just down from the Superdome. The dark green carpet was plush, the beige walls decorated with framed prints of the French Quarter, the air-conditioned atmosphere a brisk seventy degrees, smelling faintly of vanilla. The prissy, fortyish executive secretary had standard-issue icy-blonde hair, blue eyes and a chilly voice that asked, but didn't mean, "May I help you?"

Beau took his credentials from his coat pocket.

"Detective John Raven Beau. Homicide Division. I'd like to speak with Mr. Regent."

"The police?"

He opened his coat to show his badge, then showed her his weapon.

"I've got handcuffs too, if you want to see them."

"That's not necessary." The icy voice snapped as she picked up her phone receiver. "I just wanted to confirm you weren't with building security."

"No, I'm the real police."

"Mr. Regent?" Her voice softened. "A police detective would like to speak with you."

She covered her mouthpiece and asked Beau what this was about.

"Murder."

She whispered the word to Mr. Regent, hung up and asked Beau to have a seat, waving to a sofa against the far wall, adding, "It'll be a while. He's in a meeting."

"I'd rather stand here with you," Beau leaned against her desk. "I'd like to watch you work. Really. What's your name, anyway?"

Her name was Doris and she tried her best to ignore Beau, turning to her computer keyboard.

"What are you typing?" he said after she'd typed one sentence. "Anything important? You're not typing letters to the people living on Lake St. Catherine, are you?"

Doris turned her computer screen away from Beau.

"Do you have your own parking place downstairs?"

Doris glared at him.

"I had to park at a meter."

Her eyes turned to ovals and she exhaled loudly.

"Are you married?"

She stood up and moved around the desk.

"You smell nice."

She knocked softly on the large double doors that obviously hid Mr. Regent, went in and came out thirteen seconds later.

"Mr. Regent will see you now." The voice was super chilly.

"Thanks."

Mr. Regent sat alone behind a black lacquer desk the size

of Cincinnati. So much for that meeting. He was on the phone. The walls of his office were all glass, providing a dramatic look at the New Orleans skyline. Balding, Regent looked to be around fifty, with deep-set eyes, a long nose and a weak chin. If ever a face needed a beard, this was one.

Regent pointed to one of the chairs in front of his desk. Beau picked one of Regent's business cards from a silver tray on his way around the desk. Regent was Vice-President of Operations for Southeast Louisiana. Beau slipped the card into his coat pocket, as he stepped next to Regent and stared down at the uneasy oil exec, who quickly ended his call.

"I indicated for you to sit on the <u>other</u> side of my desk."

"I prefer to stand." Beau pulled out his credentials and introduced himself.

"Could you stand on the other side of my desk, please?"

The stuff Beau had learned in that body language school really worked. Americans liked to keep their space. He pulled his notebook from his pocket as he moved to the other side, giving Regent his desk as a buffer. Without looking up, Beau asked, "Where were you Saturday?"

"Why do you need to know that?"

Beau gave the man an unfriendly smile. "Don't you watch TV?"

"What?"

"It's customary for the detective to establish where everyone associated with the victim was at the time of the murder."

"What victim?"

"Eldrich Oubre." Beau watched the deep set eyes, but

Regent hid any reaction. "You know, the man Pelikan has been trying to evict from Lake St. Catherine."

Beau spotted a hint of recognition in Regent's eyes, but the man just shrugged.

"So Counselor, where were you Saturday?"

Regent pursed his lips, huffed, then explained he was home all day with his wife, cutting grass and gardening.

Beau had a hard time envisioning this guy cutting grass.

That night, Regent and his wife went to a movie.

"Where? Which movie?"

"Since when my taste in movies is the business of the police department?"

Beau waited.

"We saw <u>The Sound of Music</u> at the Prytania Theatre. It's a retrospective theatre. Know what that means, detective?"

Beau didn't snap at the bait.

"You sent Mr. Oubre several letters. Signed them yourself."

Regent shrugged again.

"We'd like to get copies of those letters."

"You cannot have them," Regent said smugly. "Those are confidential company memos."

"Then you remember them."

"I'm aware of squatters on our land on Lake St. Catherine. I sent letters to a number of people."

"Well one of them was murdered and his house burned. So you don't have to worry about him anymore."

Regent leaned back and put his hands behind his head. He was getting confident now.

"Did you ever meet Eldrich Oubre?"

"Hardly." Regent looked at his watch.

"Ever see his camp?"

"No. And this intrusion is becoming quite time-consuming. If you have a point, I wish you'd get to it, detective."

"A Pelikan crew boat was on the lake around the time of the murder. We'll need the name of the crew."

"That's confidential information. Are they suspects?"

It was Beau's turn to shrug. Then he added in a conciliatory tone, "They might have seen something. We need to talk with them."

"Good luck." Regent stood as if the interview was over. So much for being conciliatory.

Beau shot the man the look of the plains warrior – a penetrating stare with face void of expression. "Luck has nothing to do with it. I'll be back."

As he was reaching the door, Regent called out, "Expect a harder time getting past my secretary if you come back."

On Beau's way out, Doris told him, "You're a very rude young man."

Beau stopped, slipped on his Ray Bans and grinned. "I know. They teach us that at the Police Academy."

In truth, Beau learned it on the street. Years of dealing with the public.

Since it wasn't four o'clock yet, Beau hustled straight to the D.A.'s office.

TEN A.M. THE FOLLOWING MORNING, Beau and his lieutenant walked into Doris' office, with a uniformed patrolmen. Lt. Dennis Merten, two inches shorter than Beau, stood an even six-feet but looked much larger. A linebacker build, skin as dark as burned wood, Merten's wide face looked harsh, even when he smiled, which was as rare as a cool day in summer.

"Wait," Doris called out as Beau and Merten walked past her desk. "You can't go in there."

Beau smiled at the patrolman who stopped next to Doris' desk.

"I'm calling Security!" Doris snatched up her receiver.

Beau waved back at the patrolman, "Told you she was dangerous."

Regent was behind his desk again, the two chairs in front of his desk occupied by Japanese businessmen. Regent's mouth fell open, which was quickly followed by a sneer.

"How dare you!"

Beau stopped next to the Japanese businessmen, bowed slightly and said, "We're very sorry to interrupt y'all." He moved around the desk, pulling the subpoenas from an interior pocket of his tan sports jacket. Regent pushed his chair back and turned to face him.

Beau continued addressing the Japanese businessmen, "We're just the police with a subpoena for Mr. Regent here. He hasn't been very cooperative with us on a murder investigation so we're subpoenaing him and his records to the Grand Jury."

Beau dropped the subpoenas in Regent's lap. "That's a Grand Jury subpoena and a subpoena duces tecum for those letters you wrote to Mr. Oubre, the names and addresses of all crews who've worked Lake St. Catherine the last five years, especially the crew boats and all occupants the two weeks surrounding the murder, your appointment books, diaries."

Beau pointed an index finger at Regent. "See ya' Friday, Counselor."

On his way back around the huge desk, he pointed to Merten, who stood towering over Regent's visitors with a sneer on his face.

"This is my commanding officer, Lt. Merten. If you want to complain about me, this is your man."

Merten waited but Regent said nothing, so he volunteered. "Detective Beau's a little pushy sometimes, isn't he?"

"He worse than that! He's the rudest man …"

"I hear that a lot. But he's effective." Merten reached over and patted one of the startled Japanese on the shoulder. "Are <u>your</u> police officers very polite?"

The Japanese man shook his head, which brought a near-grin to Merten's face. Backing away, Merten pointed his chin toward Regent. "Next time a detective asks for your help, you might want to cooperate."

Beau led the way out. Two beefy-looking security men, in maroon sport coats, stood against the wall, the patrolman facing them with his arms folded. Beau stopped at Doris' desk, leaned both hands on top and started laughing.

"Got 'em cornered, doesn't he?"

BEAU FOUND two boys fishing from Eldrich Oubre's dock that afternoon. Both were shirtless, their brown skin shiny with perspiration. The youngest was about seven, the oldest barely a teen-ager. Their eyes widened as Beau stepped up in his shirtsleeves, badge clipped to his belt, Beretta in its canvas holster on his hip.

His smile did little to alleviate their apprehension, so Beau put his hands behind his back and asked, "Catch anything?"

The little one pointed to a green bucket. Beau looked inside and saw two perch and a nice sized largemouth bass, about three pounds.

"Very good." He stuck his hand out to the little one and said, "I'm John."

The boy shook his hand, but pulled his hand back quickly to grip his cane pole with both hands. The older boy stood and extended his hand and said he was Jeffrey. The little guy was his brother Billy.

Jeffrey carefully watched his cork as he told Beau that they lived on the other side of the levee, down the road a ways, how Mr. Oubre always let them fish from his dock when the ducks weren't around, and how sad they were about the old man.

Jeffrey's cork bobbled but went still. Beau asked his questions quietly.

The day Oubre died, Jeffrey didn't come by the camp but saw three boats on the lake, Mr. Nunez's shrimp boat, a tug boat and Pelikan's crew boat, which was the only one that came close to shore. Jeffrey said Jeansonne was nice and Eldrich Oubre was a very nice man. He steered clear of Nunez. The man ran them off once, for fishing too close to his crab traps.

"Seen any strangers around here lately?"

"Nope."

"What about hitchhikers on Highway 90?"

"Sometimes. Not lately."

Putting his sunglasses on, Beau looked toward Nunez's camp. "So Nunez's is mean, huh?"

"He yell at everybody. Even yell at Mr. Oubre cause Mr. Oubre don't want nobody putting crab traps around his dock 'cause of the ducks." Jeffrey got another nibble. When his cork stopped moving, he checked his bait and the shrimp was still there.

"You say Jeansonne's a nice man. Ever see him get mad?"

Jeffrey shook his head.

As Beau started to leave, Jeffrey landed a large sailfin catfish, about a five pounder.

"That's good eating," Beau said.

"You got that right." Jeffrey smiled broadly as he carefully worked the hook from the big cat's mouth.

Beau checked Jeansonne's camp and found no one there and the aluminum boat gone, so he headed the other direction.

Nunez's shrimp boat was a jury-rigged contraption, looked like someone nailed a couple boats together, the shrimp nets were small and all patched up, looked as if they had leprosy. His dock was in worse shape, just some rickety boards nailed together at water level.

Nunez wasn't in much better shape, a sunburned man with cotton-candy white hair and a scowling face with deep lines. He could have been younger than his sixties, but looked every bit as old as that. Nunez was using a carving knife to skin the first of two nutria hanging from an old clothes line behind his camp. A squirrel also hung from the line.

He waited until Beau was close before telling him to get off his land.

Beau tapped down his Ray Bans and gleeked the man over the top of the sunglasses. He waited for Nunez to look at him again before saying, "This isn't you land. It belongs to Pelikan Oil, doesn't it?"

Nunez looked at Beau's badge and said, "What you want with me?"

The old man pulled the guts from the nutria and dropped it in the bucket beneath the large rodent. Nutria were fair game for anyone, nowadays. Not an indigenous animal, the damn South American rodents were illegally introduced to the swamplands of south Louisiana long ago. Their only natural enemy were alligators but the nutria were too prolific to be slowed in their infestation. Cajuns ate 'em. Beau had nutria gumbo often and his father cured the pelts. Even the anti-fur people didn't complain when they started making nutria fur coats. The big, orange-toothed rodents weren't cute like mink and chinchillas.

"If you here 'bout Oubre." Nunez said. "Oil company killed him and burned his camp."

Beau pulled out his pad and pen. "Did you see it happen?"

"Don't have to." Nunez dug a small bullet from the nutria and dropped it in the bucket. "They got crew boats on the lake all the time. They think they own the land, just like Oubre thought he did."

Nunez said he wasn't around at the time of the killing. Like Jeansonne, he was out on the lake. He saw nothing, didn't even see the fire, just some smoke. When Beau asked how many letters Nunez received from Pelikan, Nunez said, "Letters?"

The old man became angry when Beau asked for his complete name, date of birth and social security number. He said he had no social security number, but provided the others before waving Beau away. He was a busy man, after all.

On his way over the levee, Beau realized there were no mailboxes along the highway. No way a postman would climb over the levee to deliver mail. Back at the office, he called Catherine and learned Pelikan delivered its letters by crew boat.

He ran the names through the police computer – Eldrich Oubre, Jacques Jeansonne, Alfonso Nunez, Jefferson D. Regent, IV, even Catherine Oubre. No hits, not even a traffic ticket except Jacques Jeansonne. Twenty-seven years earlier he was convicted of manslaughter, a barroom brawl, and spent ten years in Angola State Penitentiary.

Beau called a buddy at NOPD's Seventh District, which patrolled Highway 90 all the way to the Rigolets, and checked suspicious person reports and abandoned car reports. Only two hitchhikers were stopped in the last week, a young couple from Pennsylvania. They were searched and let go. No guns, no twenty-two. Beau checked with the state police after and came up with another big zero. The Louisiana Department of Wildlife and Fisheries hadn't any reports in the area. He didn't tell them about Nunez hunting within city limits.

Closing his eyes, Beau could see himself back in the swampland, see himself creeping around a cypress tree, getting a bead on a raccoon and shooting it with his treasured Winchester twenty-two long rifle. Subsistence living. People in the city had no idea what it was like, living off what you could kill.

Beau spent Thursday in court on an inner-city murder case from last year. A citizen named Skip Johnson had gone into Eddie's Good Luck Bar and shot one of his running pandas, Joe Bailey, three times and Bailey's girlfriend, Linda Grace, three times. Grace survived, but was paralyzed. Bailey didn't make it.

It had taken Beau three months to come up with Johnson's name from the midnight bartender at Eddie's Good Luck Bar, only the tender wouldn't testify to <u>anything</u>. It took Beau another month to get Linda Grace to confirm the story, only she also refused to testify against Johnson. They were all afraid of ole Skip Johnson. So Beau searched through armed robberies in Girt Town, where Johnson operated, and got ole Skip identified as the man who car jacked an elderly couple six months before. A search warrant of Johnson's house surfaced the gun used to kill Bailey and paralyze Linda Grace. The gun had Johnson's fingerprints on it.

Later that evening, Beau showed Grace and the reluctant

bartender his obsidian hunting knife, describing how he planned to scalp Johnson, now he was a wanted man. The next day Johnson turned himself into parish prison.

Once Skip Johnson was in jail, everyone decided to testify, especially after Beau assured them if they didn't, Johnson would be back on the street, hunting them down since Beau would tell Johnson who'd fingered him. Surprisingly, two additional eye-witnesses from the bar surfaced, all lining up to say yes, Skip Johnson shot the two. He sure did. And <u>the terror</u> of Girt Town was brought down. That was Skip Johnson's street name. He was <u>the terror</u>.

When Johnson's lawyer got to cross-examine Beau at the trial, he accused the tall detective of threatening to scalp his client.

"Didn't you threatening him with a Sioux scalping knife?"

Beau answered calmly. "It's an obsidian hunting knife and I never threatened Mr. Johnson. In fact, counselor, I never met Mr. Johnson until this morning in court. You might recall, when he turned himself in at parish prison, you ordered him not to talk with police and notified the Detective Bureau of your order."

Turning to the jury, Beau added, "My lieutenant directed me to not interview Johnson. So I never saw the man until this morning."

Beau had to wait in the hall as the line of eye-witnesses trailed into the court to hammer Skip <u>the terror</u> Johnson to the wall. In Louisiana, witnesses were sequestered. They couldn't hear other witnesses' testimony and couldn't leave the courthouse.

Sitting in the hall, Beau spotted Matt LeBlond, a Police

Association Attorney and waved him over. Short, heavy-set and balding, LeBlond looked more like an elf than a hard-nosed lawyer.

"What's up?" LeBlond's cheery personality was disarming. He was one tough bastard when pushed into a legal corner. Beau took ten minutes of his time to lay out Catherine's Oubre's potential civil case against Pelikan Oil.

LeBlond said he knew all about Louisiana's adverse possession law, his tiny eyes eager with anticipation.

"She has no money," Beau assured him.

"Yeah, but I get to sue Pelikan." LeBlond pulled out a stack of business cards and passed one of his personal cards to Beau to give to Catherine. "They'll probably settle and she'll get something," LeBlond started backing away, looking at his watch. "Have her call me."

"Thanks," Beau called out.

That's how Beau spent his Thursday.

Friday morning found him back in the criminal courts building, outside the Grand Jury room with a bespectacled assistant D. A. named Alvin Johnson (no relation to Skip <u>the terror</u>) when Jefferson D. Regent, IV, walked in with his two attorneys carrying two boxes of files and letters.

Alvin Johnson relieved the attorneys of the files and told them to take a seat in the hall. When Regent objected, Johnson grinned at him and said, "Counselor, don't you know you can't bring your lawyers into the Grand Jury?"

Beau went in and sat next to Johnson as Regent was asked one hundred and sixty-five questions, most concocted by Beau who busied himself going through the papers from the boxes. The last letter Pelikan sent to Eldrich Oubre was three weeks ago. So no crew boat delivered any letter to Oubre for weeks.

Johnson's high pitched voice grated on Beau and irritated the hell out of Regent as he asked his questions —

"Where were you on the day of Mr. Oubre's murder? What were you doing? Who from Pelikan Oil was on Lake St. Catherine on the day of the murder?" The questions continued as the A.D.A. got the names from all the crew boatmen on Lake St. Catherine for the last month, especially the ones on the lake the day of the murder.

Regent said he never met Eldrich Oubre and never been on Lake St. Catherine. He said the reason crew boats were on the lake was to survey their land. Geologists were on most boats. No one carried weapons on Pelikan crew boats.

Those were the pertinent questions. The remaining one hundred plus were to piss Regent off, like when he was born, where, how long had he been a vice-president at Pelikan, was he related to anyone else at Pelikan, how many other people had he forced off their land, and did he know a woman named Judith "Bunny" Jones, a prostitute who dealt with high-paying clientele. Regent tried to remain cool as Johnson ran off a litany of other names of prostitutes and drug dealers names, asking Johnson if he knew them. He simmered, but didn't lose his cool. Beau was happy just to see him simmer.

THE COVE at the University of New Orleans was a mini-food court with fast food outlets and a couple homemade cookeries. Seated at a rear table, Catherine Oubre wore a white tee-shirt and jeans and looked as young as a high-school student. Beau, in his gray suit, was thankful for the brisk air-conditioning. Catherine's eyes looked particularly dark in the dim light.

Over steakburgers, Beau told Catherine what he'd learned from Mr. Regent, which wasn't much, and what he'd learned from the boat crew he'd interviewed the previous evening.

The captain of the boat on the lake on the day her father died was a retired New Orleans fireman, friendly as hell, answering Beau's questions without hesitation. The crew had two retired sheriff's deputies. They didn't see Oubre that day, never went within a mile of Oubre's camp. Despite Regent's statement, crew boats usually have weapons on board, twenty-twos mostly. That day the captain brought a shotgun to use on water moccasins. He didn't know if anyone else had a weapon aboard.

"The captain was aware of Pelikan's feud with your father, but never spoke with your father personally. He said your Daddy always waved when the crew boat passed and the captain waved back."

Catherine put her burger down and dabbed her mouth with the napkin and just stared at Beau with a sadness in her eyes.

"Do you really think you'll catch who did it?"

"Yes," he answered evenly, then took a bite of burger, which was quite good, nice an spicy.

"You sound pretty sure of yourself. You know something you're not telling me?"

Beau looked into her eyes again and said, "I'll solve it because I won't stop until I do. I didn't say I'd solve it quickly."

Catherine picked up her burger and took a bite. "What will you do next?"

"I went through the papers provided by Pelikan and found the letters they sent your father and Jeansonne."

"Find anything interesting?" Catherine picked up a French fry and nibbled at it.

"It's what I didn't find. No letter to Nunez."

"I wonder why."

"That's what I wondered and went back and checked the description of your father's land. Did you know he claimed three miles of land heading northeast from his camp?"

Catherine shook her head.

"Nunez's camp is on your father's land. And one other thing," he said. "Jeansonne served ten years in Angola for manslaughter."

Catherine took in a deep breath and held it for a long while.

JEANSONNE WASN'T HOME that afternoon. Beau snooped around and found two wet cast nets out back. Jeansonne had been there, unless someone else hung up his nets. So he headed for Nunez's.

As he crested the levee behind Nunez's camp, he spotted the old man walking away from his clothes line where three fresh nutria hung. Nunez carried an orange bucket over to a smaller, metal bucket. He reached in and pulled entrails from the orange bucket and dropped them into the metal bucket, before tossing the rest of the blood on the grass. The entrails would make good crab bait.

Beau moved down the levee. Nunez saw him, picked up the metal bucket and headed for his boat. He took off before Beau reached his camp. Wiping the perspiration from his forehead, Beau looked back at the nutria and felt a tingling in the soles of his feet.

He felt his heart racing as he stepped over to the slop Nunez had just thrown out. Two shiny bullets lay in the bloody grass. Beau went down on his haunches and picked up the pellets. They were in pretty good shape. He could clearly see the lands and grooves carved into the bullets as they traveled through the barrel of Nunez's gun.

<u>You never know</u>, told himself as he stood up with the pellets. *Sometimes you have to make your own luck.*

He slipped the pellets into a brown evidence envelope from his trunk, then wiped off his hands with one of disposable wipes he kept to clean his sunglasses.

THE LEAD OFFICER of the Special Response Team, which used to be called SWAT, notified headquarters on the radio, said they were at Lake Catherine. A native New Orleanian, the leader used the colloquial name for the lake. On maps, it may be Lake St. Catherine, but to locals it's Lake Catherine. Beau was still learning colloquialisms and made note.

Armed with search warrants for Nunez's camp and boat and an arrest warrant, Beau led four uniformed officers across the levee, just as the sun began its final descent in the western sky, shimmering orange on the brown water of Lake St. Catherine. Three white egrets flew over the policemen as they reached the camp.

Nunez's boat wasn't there. The door was locked but a side window was unlocked so Beau climbed in and let the others inside. He spotted Nunez's rifle in a far corner. It was a cheap, single shot Ivor Johnson twenty-two long rifle, Li'l Champ model.

Beau greeted an angry Nunez with a cold smile when the old man stormed up the stairs of his camp an hour later, the same smile that crossed Beau's face when the firearms examiner told him, yes, the bullets he'd brought in came from the gun which killed Eldrich Oubre.

"What the hell is all this?" Nunez shouted.

Beau grabbed the old man by the shoulder, spun him around, patted him down, and handcuffed him behind his back before Nunez could get another angry sentence out.

"What the hell's going on?" Nunez yelled again.

Beau pulled his Miranda Rights card from his credentials pouch and read Nunez his rights, then told him he was under arrest for the murder of Eldrich Oubre. Nunez stiffened and looked away from Beau and never said another word until they were in the interview room at the Detective Bureau.

"Who saw me?" Nunez asked as Beau turned on the video camera to get his statement on tape. He asked the same question again as soon as Beau finished reading him his right, again.

"Who do you think saw you?"

"Those damn kids. They keep ruining my crab traps, trying to fish. Got the whole goddamn lake to fish and they come by me."

"Did you see them before or after you killed Mr. Oubre?"

"I didn't see them," Nunez's voice lowered. "But they always snoopin' around."

For the next two hours Beau had to do an unpleasant thing. He had to be nice to a killer, had to be actually friendly. The jury would see how friendly and know Nunez wasn't forced to confess. It wasn't easy for Beau at first, but he began to see something of his father in the old man, although his father never lived to be that old. Cigarettes cut short Calixte Beau's life.

Maybe it was way Nunez tilted his head when he spoke, or the way he brushed his fingers up and down the inside of his arm, from wrist to elbow joint. Beau found his questions, although just as pointed, didn't sound as tough. His voice didn't have that edge, although he kept his face expressionless, like a good plains warrior.

He focused on something Nunez said at their first meeting, something about how Pelikan thought they owned the land, <u>just like Oubre thought he did</u>. Nunez became agitated, Oubre's claim on his land pissed him of.

When pressed Nunez said he couldn't explain how it happened. It just did.

"He was out on his dock, feeding his damn ducks when I pulled up in my boat and he yelled at me, then walked away, told me to go away. I followed him. Shot him through the screen door when he turned around. Then I burned the place."

The old man's face was flushed. "I don't know why I did it. I just lost it, went crazy when he walked away like that."

Beau went over it again, in more detail, so the jury wouldn't miss anything. His voice lost its gentleness when Nunez said Eldrich Oubre caused his own death, not letting Nunez set his crab traps near his camp.

Stepping back into the Detective Bureau squad room, Beau found a note from the D.A.'s office taped to his desk. Skip Johnson, AKA: <u>the terror</u>, was convicted of second degree murder. It was the best the state could hope for – a life sentence with no parole, probation, or commutation of sentence. Unless he escaped or got a presidential pardon, Skip Johnson's days of terrorizing Gert Town were over.

A SNOWY EGRET stood on one leg at the edge of Lake St. Catherine, just down from Eldrich Oubre's burned camp. Studying the water so intently, it didn't notice Beau walk past. It was too used to humans.

Not a good idea, Beau thought.

Catherine was standing on her father's dock with a bag of popcorn. She dropped popcorn in a slow circle for the mallards and a couple white ducks. The strong afternoon sun went right through her loose-fitting, white cotton dress and for a moment Beau could see the outline of her body through the cloth.

She turned to him and he took off his sunglasses and had to squint now. Catherine smiled sadly and sucked in a deep breath.

"You really did it," she said as he stepped up.

Beau put his sunglasses back on.

"How did you figure it out?"

"By not trying to figure it out," he said.

Her brow furrowed, so he went on. "T.V. detectives look around for suspects and go after them. We don't. We just keep gathering data, gathering evidence until it brings us to the killer. All I did was gather."

Catherine still stared at him, so Beau took his glasses off again. It was rarely this easy, Beau was going to tell her, but the word "easy" caught in his throat. There was nothing easy about a father's murder.

"Did he tell you why?"

"I don't think he even knows why. He said he just lost it. He has an anger inside and it built until he snapped."

"That lawyer called me. He thinks I have a good case. Good enough to force Pelikan to settle."

Beau was glad LeBlond followed right up on it.

Catherine turned the popcorn bag upside down and shook it, scattering popcorn on the murky water, some kernels falling on the ducks. She folded the popcorn bag carefully, then folded her arms.

"Looks like my daddy's gonna leave me enough money to get a good start in life," she said. Catherine bowed her head and took in another deep breath. A moment later a tear fell on the dock.

Beau wanted to put his arms around her, pull her close, but knew better.

After a minute, Catherine composed herself and said, "Too bad we can't get to know each other better. And you know what I mean. I could see it in your eyes the first time I looked into them."

Beau felt his heartbeat rising.

Catherine wiped the tears from her eyes and looked into his eyes.

"Every time I'd see you, I'd think of this," she said.

He nodded.

"Can I catch a ride back in with you?"

"Sure."

Beau took a step away but stopped as Catherine took another long look out at the still water. Beau closed his eyes and concentrated on the familiar scent of salt water mud for a moment.

"I can't come back here again," she said, her voice choked with emotion.

Beau understood exactly what she meant as he led her back across to the levee. He had said the same goodbye to Vermilion Bay years ago.

LISA DANNY-ROBERTS

Lisa Danny-Roberts is a retired lawyer who seems to be active in a lot of the arts, including her writing. This is her first story in these pages, but I sure hope it won't be the last.

Lisa manages in very quick order to paint an image of Los Angeles during the Santa Ana winds and of a woman who knows the city.

OPEN ALL NIGHT

LISA DANNY-ROBERTS

A strong wind blows through the night. A Santa Ana wind, hot, sticky, relentless. The devils breath her mother called it. Las Angelenos hated it. It was hard to breathe, made you itchy like ants were scurrying around your skin. By the second week, mothers began back handing mild mannered children for spilling milk, then starred at their hand in disbelief.

She grunted as she opened the window all the way. No screen, she leaned onto the sill and stared out, 2:31am. The streetlights ten feet apart light the road like Christmas. Angelenos were terrified of crime. They believed illuminating the darkness would keep them safe from Manson, the night stalker, the serial killer du jour. Los Angeles could always count on having at least one serial killer, there are always slain and missing girls. They are necessary to feed the tv anchors, influencers, podcasters.

A million-dollar industry feeding on morbid curiosity and

despair. The street lights obliterate the stars giving the night an eerie glow. The insistent whine of a siren. The neighbors black lab has been barking all night. He too restless and wary. There was the jumping blur of images from the Nelson's bay window across the street. Harold must have fallen asleep with the tv on. A rap song with a continuous beat and haughty anger provided a sound track. Los Angeles refused to sleep, stuck in a restless collective waiting. Yearning for the wind to disappear and leave them alone in their smog and sunshine.

Emily stares at the ceiling and listens to David snore. She gives up trying to sleep, throws off the covers, pulls on her jeans and a hoodie, slips on her tennis shoes. She doesn't bother to brush her long blonde hair or wash the sleep out of her eyes. She closes the bedroom door softly behind her.

Her feet know the route, she walks it in the dark often. She turns right at the corner and walks three blocks. She grabs the sticky metal handle, pulls open the door. She blinks from the glare of the fluorescent lights. The convenience store is crowded with lottery ticket advertisements, girls dressed in pink skimpy outfits stare out from the covers of Korean magazines.

Soda flavors of melon and blueberry fill the refrigerator. Bags of lichee nuts and seaweed chips line the shelves. The store is small and narrow. Cardboard boxes fill the floor, some coated with a thin film of grey dust.

Behind the counter Will looks up from his book. Tall, thin with brown hair, dark eyes, bright smile. His shoulders are relaxed, jaw unclenched. She likes this Will better than the tense one she is used to.

"Santa Anas are still with us." he says closing his book.

"Can't sleep," she shrugs.

"You and half of the city. It will cool down soon and then you will sleep."

They both know he is being kind. She doesn't sleep much. She grabs an empty plastic milk crate turns it on its side grabs a Diet Pepsi, then sits down on the far side of the counter. From months of practice, she knows how to perfectly balance on the small surface of the milk crate.

"What are you reading?"

He holds up a paperback with a heavily armed soldier on the cover.

"It's great to read for pleasure again. When I picked up the book I grabbed a yellow highlighter to take notes, then realized I could just read it and enjoy it and not have to remember anything."

She smiles, he is waiting for bar results. He took the three-day test months ago and still has to wait six more weeks for results.

Every day he waits must seem like a year. Lately, he seems calm, enjoying the break, allowing himself to relax after three grueling years of study.

"How are you?"

She shrugs, unsure if she wants to talk tonight. Some nights they chatter for hours, other nights, she drinks her Diet Pepsi while he sits and reads. She has never seen a customer in the store, she wonders why the owner pays to keep it open all night.

The store feels safe, far removed from everyday life. She wants to tell him. She knows that once the words come out of her mouth it will be real.

"You have six more weeks to wait, are you going on a vacation, something you enjoy?"

"I always wanted to see the backwaters. Up near Minnesota, miles and miles of rivers and no one around." He looks through the front window as if he can see the river flowing outside the door.

"Sounds great, when would you go?"

"Haven't decided yet, I can go anytime."

The thought of him leaving splits her in two. She looks forward to being here in the middle of the night, the two of them in their own world. There is an intimacy about it she has never felt with David.

"I couldn't have gotten through the bar without you."

"I didn't do anything."

"Whenever I got tired and discouraged, you told me I could do it."

"You can," she smiles.

He looks at her pale drawn face, the purple under each eye like bruises. Each time she comes in she looks more haggard. Her straight dirty blonde hair sticking to the sides of her head. Hazel eyes puffy from lack of sleep. Thin lips in a perpetual frown. She looks like a forty-year-old single mother beaten down by life. Not the happy 31-year-old he knows.

"When are you going to tell me what's wrong?"

"It's a long story."

He glances at the clock. "It's 3:38 a.m., I don't get off until 6:00 a.m. I have time for a very long story."

"For Christmas my sister Janice gave everyone in the family a DNA test. She said her neighbor did it and found out she was ¾ Scottish. I don't understand why anyone would care. Janice has to keep up with her neighbors. My mom and my brother and Janice took the kits home, filled out the papers, spit into the boxes, sent them to the company. I didn't do it. I like my privacy. What happens if Amazon buys the company, then they have my DNA? Who knows what they will use it for? Janice kept calling and texting, you're the only one who hasn't done it." Emily shakes her head.

"Like it was a test and not a present. Like I had no choice."

"Did you finally give in?"

"No, I didn't. She had a family party, kept a Diet Pepsi can I held. Paid extra to have them lift the DNA off it. She forged my signature on the forms then sent it in. I didn't know anything about it. About two months ago, I get this letter, you know the type, big bold letters open immediately."

"The type everyone throws away first."

She nods. "I threw it away. They kept coming and finally one came that needed a signature. I went down to the post office to sign for it. It was from this company Ancestry 230. It had the results of my test.

I share family DNA with my mother, but not my father. My mother had an affair. I have no idea who my father is."

"Must have been rough to find out."

"Honestly, I wasn't that surprised. I'm the youngest, my father always treated me like an afterthought. Janice was always perfect and I could never do anything right. Everything made a weird kind of sense."

"Do you think he knew?"

"I think he must have suspected, doesn't matter, he died two years ago. The letter went on to say they found a genetic abnormality. They suggested I get genetic counseling and testing as soon as possible. It had a phone number to a testing site."

She swallows a mouthful of Diet Pepsi, "I thought it was all bs, just another way to scare me and make money. I shoved the letter in a drawer and forgot all about it. A few months ago, I started getting nose bleeds, thought the air was just dry. They didn't go away. went to my doctor, took the letter. I took a bunch of tests."

She stares at the red letters on the Diet Pepsi can, turns it slowly. Takes a deep breath, looks up hesitates, not wanting to make it real. "I have Huntington's Chorea." She has said it out loud. It is out. She looks around the store and starts to laugh.

"I have Huntington's chorea and I told you in a Korean convenience store."

He moves under the camera, throws a hand towel over the lens. Comes around the corner gets on his knees behind her. Wraps both his arms around her. She leans back into him. She cries softly, tears drip onto his arms.

She stops. He gets up walks back around the counter.

"I'm so sorry," she says.

"Why are you sorry?"

"I shouldn't burden you with this."

"How long before it gets really bad?"

"They don't know for sure, I have a very severe case, some people live with it for years, but they think I have about two years."

"What did David say?"

" I didn't tell him."

He cocks his head, gives her a puzzled look.

"He has been so cold and distant lately, I think he has been having an affair."

"An affair, you have only been married a year and a half."

"I think he regrets getting married. He has a way of making me feel bad about everything. Somehow he is going to make this all my fault."

"Sounds like you married a narcissistic asshole." He says before he can stop himself. He waits for her to defend him.

"Yes I did," she agrees.

They sit in silence. Listening to the hum from the lights, the drone of the refrigerator motors.

"Why don't you come with me on my vacation?"

"I can't just leave my life."

"Why not?"

"What about my family? It would put them through hell."

"Probably."

She is small, petite, blonde. A media darling. In her mind she sees the posters, the choked sobs in the tv appearances. Janice coming alive in the spotlight, having to be reminded to look sad. Her brother Ben refusing to leave work because he is just so busy. Her mother lost, hiding her secrets. David number one suspect, his mistress exposed to the world. Screw em she thinks as a delicious wickedness spreads through her.

"You don't want to take care of me."

"Why don't we go to on vacation for a while and see how we feel after that?"

She looks down at her torn jeans, pink hoody, white tennis shoes.

"I don't have anything. Not even my phone."

His brows furrow, she feels his mind racing, trying on then discarding possibilities.

"Perfect, no phone to trace."

"What will we do for money?" she asks.

" I have a little bit saved, and I just got a $5000 check as a graduation present from my uncle."

He gets up, pulls the towel off the camera and uses it to polish the camera lens. Puts the towel down on the counter.

"You will get in trouble. The police will find camera footage from all the times I've been in."

He shakes his head. "We only keep it a week, you haven't been in for about ten days, should be okay."

In that instant they become coconspirators. In a soft whisper he says, "Go use the bathroom, come out look directly into the camera, pay for your Pepsi and snacks. Go out the door, pretend you have to tie your shoe. Tie it, look up directly into the camera outside the door. Walk down the street. Two blocks down is a bus stop, it is 5:38 a.m. A bus should be by in about ten minutes. It will take you to Hamilton Street. Get off the bus, walk left, away from the bus, to the strip mall. Turn right, at the very end of the mall is a

Mexican restaurant. Anita's, I eat there often, the owner can't afford a camera. Wait for me."

She nods, looks up at the camera walks out the door. She follows his directions, gets on the crowded, dirty bus. Finds Anita's. The restaurant has six Formica tables with wooden chairs. Menu is on the chalkboard behind the counter. Items are written in Spanish with English underneath. Coffee is brewing in a large pot on the counter.

"Hola" says the woman behind the counter. She has a round face. Her big grin shows missing teeth. Her black hair pulled back in a tight pony tail. She could be forty or sixty.

She points at the coffee pot. Emily nods her head. She goes and pours herself a cup, adds milk. Sits down at the table watches as the workers scurry around in the kitchen.

Will waves as he comes through the back screen door. He grabs the woman at the counter in a bear hug. She hugs him back, kisses both cheeks. He bends down, presses something in her hand. He puts his finger to his lips. She nods.

He beckons to Emily. She walks toward him. Together they walk out the back door into the morning. He grabs her hand as they walk down a street full of manicured lawns and huge stone porches.

She opens the door to his car, slides into the front seat. At 6:24 a.m. on a Thursday morning Emily Hawkins becomes one of LA's missing. At this time tomorrow the media frenzy will begin.

K.A. WIGGINS

This is K.A. Wiggins's second story in these pages, following her amazing story last month. This month it is the first paragraph of this story that just yanked me in and would not let me go.

K.A. Wiggins (Kaie) is an award-winning Canadian speculative fiction author, speaker, and creative writing coach known for the celebrated gothic-dystopian YA Dark Fantasy series Threads of Dreams.

She writes across fantasy, science fiction, and horror subgenres (often within the same work) for middle grade (forthcoming), young adult, and all-ages/adult audiences, exploring the tangled webs of society, environment, and identity through intricate, dreamlike tales of monsters and magic. For more on her work go to her website at https://kawiggins.com

CHILDREN OF EARTH

K.A. WIGGINS

The toe wiggled at Mirella from the compost heap. She let the lid drop with a thud and backed out of the cloud of flies. Enough. Time to order an electronic composter.

When she'd committed to living zero waste for a year, she'd promised herself she wouldn't be one of those bougie millennials buying sculpted glass jars and clean, Nordic-looking wood everything to support the lifestyle. No, she was going legit. Pure. Capitalism wasn't going to benefit from her efforts to renew the planet.

But the toe had broken her. And it was worth a couple hundred bucks to incinerate it in an appropriately eco-friendly fashion. Though the advertising didn't call it incinerating, of course. It was a "countertop appliance designed to speed-compost household waste with no mess, no fuss, and no odour."

Did she believe the ad copy? Hardly. It'd probably be

stinky, loud, dirty, and leer accusingly at her across her open plan living space with its one glowing eye that doubled as a magic button for everything she could ever need the space-age convenience to do, because heaven forbid they design machines with actual control panels these days.

Mirella paused at the final step of the online order form, chewing over her options. The breadmaker-sized unit would undoubtedly come with its own set of waste-generating challenges. Plastic film, packing peanuts, even cardboard. Although, as far as the cardboard went, she could probably cut it up small and practice using the composter to dispose of it as a trial run before taking on the toe.

She'd tried flushing the clippings at first, reasoning that it was just another type of biological waste, and it wasn't as if she was going to start collecting all the *other* types for in-home composting. That was probably illegal, anyway. Hazardous waste, or something. Wasn't that how they got plagues, and dysentery, and all sorts of old-fashioned or other-country-type diseases, back in the day?

But that was before Mirella had read an article on how some mineral or something in human hair was great for house plants and had had the bright idea of tucking nail clippings as well as snarls of hair into the dirt like a twisted Halloween version of those cute little plastic stakes from the dollar store where you were supposed to write the plant's name in calligraphy or some shit. Not that she shopped at dollar stores. That would be very wrong.

Anyway, she hadn't realized she had a problem until the leaves on her test plant started getting a little too silky and the petals opened to keratinous hearts. She'd pulled on her ethically-harvested natural latex gloves and yanked the poor thing out by the roots, cramming it headfirst into the steel pail she used as a temporary compostables receptacle, before emptying it into the biweekly pickup bins outside. After a moment's consideration, she'd upended the pot and emptied the soil into the pail as well.

When the pot had been well scrubbed with an organic coconut-shell-fibre-and-wire brush and her pulse had settled back to its usual serene pace, Mirella had even been able to chuckle at her overactive imagination. Poor plant. All the same, she'd stick to flushing all biological waste in future. In-home circular economies were all well and good, but clearly she'd crossed some kind of mental barrier and should back away slowly.

Mirella had dreamed of toenail-lined sewage pipes and flowers unfurling to display eyeballs and ears and tiny little baby hands waving at her, and woke with a dull sense of dread. It had worsened when she realized she'd neglected to wash out the little glass-and-tin box she carried her lunches in over the weekend. The remnants of Friday's organic, locally grown and sustainably harvested meal were gently growing local, presumably organic, and clearly wildly sustainable green-and-white fuzz.

She'd ignored it in favour of coffee—not locally grown, unfortunately, but purchased from some kind of collective that ensured farmers got paid and didn't clear more rainforest to grow the beans or use pesticides. At least, that's what they'd claimed at the refillery where they'd smiled indulgently at her stained yogurt container and gingerly slid scoops of beetle-shiny beans in. The customer waiting behind her had been less gentle in her judgment.

Mirella had smiled with tight lips and clenched teeth all through the lecture on the dangers of chemical-leeching plastics making her stupid, infertile, and fat. She'd nodded, eyed the aesthetically-pleasing display of glass-and-cork and ceramic coffee storage containers, the hand-lettered pottery studio tag matching the logo emblazoned across the lecturing woman's allegedly-ocean-reclaimed-plastic tote bag, and brightly thanked the now-ranting woman for sharing her knowledge before taking her plastic-encased beans and running. Maybe she'd go back to refilling at the local grocery's bulk section. Though their selection was limited and probably not organic, much less ethical, whatever the labels claimed.

Mirella sighed and knocked the puck of gently steaming grounds into her compostables pail. The toenails recoiled in pain. All three of them.

She could have sworn that she'd buried the suspicious-looking flowers at the bottom of the pail under a full pot's worth of dirt, but now the gently curved pinkish nails they'd grown were attached to scraps of flesh. Presumably complete with tendons and nerve endings buried somewhere in the dirt, given the flinch.

Mirella might've yelped, or screamed, or sworn—but she'd caught sight of her neighbour through the small above-sink window in her kitchen. He was just returning from a jog in his heat-molded algae, ethically harvested wool, and recycled pop bottle runners, looking sweaty but perfect in the kind of merino athletic gear that was well beyond her budget. A passing conversation last fall had led to her growing aware-ness of the importance—no, the imperative—of committing to a sustainable lifestyle. Which she had done. Was doing. However . . .

She looked down in despair. They shared a bin for compost pickup. It was the highlight of her week, politely fighting over who would deliver it to the curb, then wheeling the hip-high bin back to its home beside his coach house unit, where she could peek in the windows and pretend she, too, lived in an Instagram-worthy snap of eco-friendly domestic bliss, instead of a dank half-basement.

But now what? She could hardly sully their shared bin with her nightmarish leavings. And what if he *saw*? He might come loping out on those long, impeccably clad legs with a late addition of coffee grounds, or the faded and limp leavings of post-soup-stock vegetable trimmings, only to be confronted with a crop of toes waggling back at him.

No, she couldn't bear it. He'd never look at her the same way. If he ever looked at her.

That was when she'd thought up the compost heap. It'd

been brilliant, really. How better to bask in his attention than a joint project? And when he'd bowed out only a day after helping her mark and measure the patch of shared yard for the heap, she'd understood, she really had. He had important work to do. Planet-saving work, something with research and complicated plans and lots of travel, carefully offset with carbon credits when he couldn't walk, cycle, or take public transit, of course.

So she'd ferreted out a series of free video explainers, sourced and hauled the materials home, and knocked up the frame for a backyard compost heap on her own. She'd emptied her now-ripe-and-wriggly compostables pail into the bottom and covered it in the proscribed layers, careful to bury the evidence from view. Down at the bottom, it'd surely suffocate. Whatever *it* was.

That had been two weeks ago. Mirella shuddered at the thought of what else hid just beneath the surface. She'd only spotted one toe, but the others couldn't be far behind. Whispering up an apology to Mother Earth, or whoever interceded on behalf of reluctant polluters, she went back a few steps and clicked the overnight delivery option on the home composter. It would be a little worse for the planet, but much, much better for her peace of mind and chances of domestic bliss with Mr. Eco-Everything.

In the meantime, she'd just have to stake out the compost heap.

"Gardening?" he'd asked, taking in her thrifted straw hat, the undyed (and, as yet, uncreased) organic cotton gloves clutched in one hand, and rusted steel trowel at her feet.

She'd nodded, speechless. Then she spotted the pail in his hands.

"Let me," she'd managed, stuttering a little on that first L, tripping over the trowel in her hurry to place herself between him and the compost heap.

He blinked, tightening his grip. His pail gleamed, the outside beaten copper, undoubtedly from some far-away women's collective or artisanal workshop, free of drips or stains.

Mirella grimaced at the dirt under her nails—not from gardening, she'd just been afraid to cut them for so long she didn't have a brush with long enough bristles to clean underneath—but held out her hands anyway, in what she hoped was a charming manner. "It's no trouble."

Her neighbour chewed his lip, a little flushed, his gaze flickering from the compost heap to her and back.

"Actually," he said, his perfect voice just on the edge of breathless. "Actually, I think I forgot—"

"What have you got there, Jason?" a woman's voice trilled, too bright.

Mirella backed against the compost heap and sat with a thump. It was the local artisanal pottery lecturer from the zero waste refillery. Of course it was.

"Karen," Jason said with relief, turning away from Mirella and her buzzing, stinking seat. He all but jogged over and leaned in, as if for a kiss.

Karen leaned away. "Don't let me stop you." She eyed the pail clutched in his white-nailed, tendon-ridged hands.

Mirella closed her eyes. Then she hopped up from her seat. "Let me get that for you. No, it's no trouble at all—"

She brushed past Jason's objections, shouldering Karen to one side, and seized the pail. He didn't let go. If anything, he pulled it closer, cuddling it like a small animal or a favourite toy. Mirella came with it, her pulse racing at the proximity, the heat of his body, the clean scent of—

She wrinkled her nose. She knew that smell. He'd left his compostables pail too long without emptying it and it had started growing fungus, or mold, or whatever it was that happened when you let food scraps sit long enough to not only rot but generate completely new organisms, complete with rainbow-hued fur.

Was that what this was about? He was embarrassed it had taken him—Mr. Perfect Eco Saint—too long to empty his compost pail and the results were toxic to anyone within a ten-foot radius? He'd been travelling recently; it's not like anyone would blame him.

"It's okay," Mirella murmured so Karen wouldn't hear. "I *know*. I get it. Just leave it with me."

Jason blanched, his handsome features going a sickly pale green, eyes widening, dampening. He looked like he was about to cry. Then his gaze shifted, focusing on something past her shoulder. His expression smoothed to genial blandness. "No, no. I've got it."

He stepped back, turning on his heel, clearly intending to break Mirella's hold. She wasn't expecting it. Off-balance, she staggered, her weight falling to one side, both arms firmly locked around the spotless copper pail. She pulled Jason off balance, their legs tangling, eyes widening, breaths merging, a startled shout subsumed into a wordless burst of air as elbows and hips and ribs collided with the earth.

And, at the same moment, a slight but audible *pop* and a roiling wave of noxious fumes sent Mirella rolling away from what might otherwise have been a thoroughly enjoyable entanglement.

On hands and knees she coughed, eyes watering. In the periphery of her vision, Jason stiffened, moaned, and went limp.

"What is *that*?" came Karen's strident voice. Then, a moment later. "That's *not* what I think it is. Jason?"

His arms lift as if in wordless plea, falter, and fold to cover his face. "This isn't a good time, Karen."

She sniffed. "When is? Look, I'm a busy woman. I have goals. A business to run. And I can't have my brand sullied by whatever *this* is. You can keep your weird little hobbies to yourself."

Jason nodded without uncovering his face. "Yes, a hobby," he said tonelessly.

Karen's muttering about closet creeps and unproductive use of time receded into the distance. Mirella crawled a couple feet before attempting her feet.

"Sorry." She stared at the peeling siding to avoid facing Jason. "I didn't mean to—"

"I'll move," he said quickly. "You'll never have to see me again. And it's not—it's really not like it looks like, okay? Like Karen said, just a hobby. You don't need to call the police—"

Police? Mirella swung around in surprise. She left her mouth hanging open despite the truly horrifying taste of the fumes. Slimy, rotten scraps were smeared across Jason's chest. It was foul-looking and smelling, but nothing criminal. Sure, he shouldn't have bought more kale than he could finish. She suspected that larger chunk was a beef bone, and everyone knew feedlots were bad for the environment, but he'd probably sourced it from one of those grass-fed, free-range, carbon-sequestering herds, or whatever. And, while those baby carrots looked a little pale, they were probably still edible—

One moved. Bent and wriggled. Mirella took a step forward. Then another, ignoring the stench to examine the offending scrap. A thick, pinkish-pale, shell-like arc, capped with a translucent whitish strip and set into a stubby, mottled—

"Where did you get that?" she demanded, her gut churning.

Jason followed her stare, groaned, and covered his face again.

Mirella crouched down. Reached. Hesitated.

He'd been in the compost pile. The toe she'd spotted hadn't been the first after all. But why had he taken in inside? And, if he'd wanted it for something, why was it in his compostables pail and headed back to the heap?

The big toe flexed again, inching out from under a strip of banana peel. The others, smaller, rocked and wriggled sleepily like a litter of kittens waking from a nap. Mirella gasped at the wiry dark hairs dusting their knuckles. Or whatever it was you called the bendy bits of toes. Her hair was a pale brown, mousy-ash and near-invisible against her skin. And she most certainly did not grow hair on her toes. At least, not that much.

"Where did you get that?" she asked again in a whisper.

"It's moving, isn't it?" Jason moaned. He peeked between

his fingers at her. "Would you believe it's a hobby? I, um. I make tiny marionettes out of vegetable scraps. Lifelike, isn't it?"

The toe flexed again, dragging itself fully out from under the banana peel. Was that bone at the end? Why didn't it bleed?

"Oh, um. That one's animatronic," he gulped, fingers fluttering above the toe as if afraid to touch it.

Mirella went and found her now crumpled and grass-stained gloves and handed them to him. He nodded his thanks, tucked as much of his long fingers as would fit inside their protection, and gingerly lifted the offending digit. It flexed with noticeable irritation.

"There's something you should see," Mirella said, taking a deep breath. Then she doubled over, coughing.

"Sorry," Jason muttered. "I didn't want to—I mean, I meant to—"

"Seriously, just get over here." Eyes watering, she grabbed his arm and dragged him, food scraps and animate digits peeling off with every step, to the compost heap. She grimaced, one hand on the lid. He'd never see her the same way. If she did this, she was outing herself as possibly the most disgusting person on the planet. Her toenail clippings were so gross they'd straight-up come back to life after being buried. Reanimated toes. Who knew what was next? Would they regenerate a full eco-zombie-copy of her, or just keep spreading until they took over the planet in endless, wriggling pink fields?

"I should . . . I should go," Jason said, tugging against her grip, a clone of what could only be his big toe squirming in one hand. "I need to wash. And pack. If there are any countries you'd like to visit in the future, just let me know and I'll steer clear."

"You don't need to go," Mirella said. And, staring right up into his beautiful, shame-filled eyes, she flung up the lid covering the compost heap.

A burst of flies heralded the start of their domestic bliss.

After he'd gotten over the first wave of shock and disgust, Jason had gently nestled his toes, one by one, between hers and covered them in the scraps they'd gathered together from his shirt, trousers, and the trampled yard. He'd closed the lid gently and tried to kiss her before remembering a shower was in order.

She moved into the coach house that night and never left, keeping her dark and dingy semi-underground suite for the children's sake. It turned out the two most disgusting people on the planet were 100% compatible in biologically and emotionally fascinating ways. The toes proliferated. But they also collaborated. And, in the cozy dark heat of the backyard compost heap, they merged to grow something beautiful.

Jason joked about naming the first one Karen.

Mirella sent the automatic composter back.

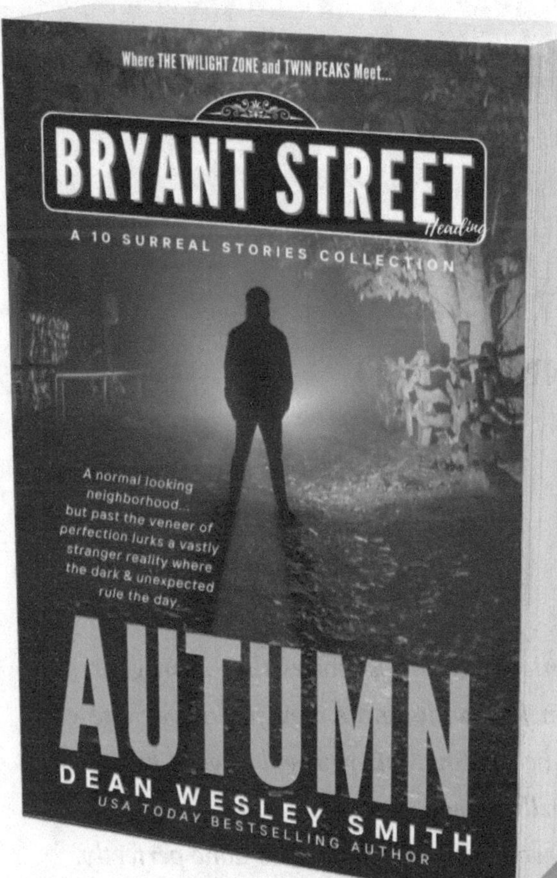

Where
THE TWILIGHT ZONE
Lives...

wmgbooks.com

ANNIE REED

Professional writer Annie Reed writes stories that span genres and are always powerful. In fact with Annie, you just never know the type of story you might be reading, but you will always know it will grab you and be a compelling read.

This story of a heist is a wonderful example. And done perfectly.

So far Annie has had a story in every issue of this magazine and as the editor, I hope to continue that streak.

Annie's stories have appeared in four best mystery stories of the year volumes so far. Look for so much more of Annie's work at her website https://anniereed.wordpress.com/

THE WHITE WHALE

ANNIE REED

Edgar should have expected the knock, but the sudden sharp rap on his front door still made him jump.

His apartment building had been new back when he was still just a gleam in his daddy's eye, and that was nearly three-quarters of a century ago. The knock made the old warped door rattle in its frame.

Back in the day, he'd had nerves of steel. Now the sudden sound made the paintbrush twitch in his hand, leaving a blotch of sepia on the canvas where only lavender and pale blue should have been.

"Son of a bitch," he muttered as he peered at the painting he'd been futzing with on and off for over a week. Mostly off. His arthritis had been flaring up thanks to the recent cold snap.

Today had been a good day to paint. He'd been making decent progress putting brush to canvas, bringing to life old

179

memories of the lake where he'd spent his honeymoon with his blushing bride, God rest her soul. He could let the sepia dry and paint over it, but he didn't want to stop. He was too old to waste time waiting for paint to dry.

He put down his palette and dunked the brush in the tin can half filled with paint thinner. The apartment smelled of paint thinner and oil paint and coffee. Good smells. His doctor had wanted him to give up coffee and cigarettes. Edgar figured he was batting .500 by giving up cigarettes. A better average than the Yankees, and besides, what was the point of living if you couldn't enjoy it?

The knock came again. Edgar knew who it had to be without even looking through the peephole.

"Hold your horses," he said as he wiped his hands on a paint-stained towel.

Not one of Millie's fancy towels. He kept those in the bottom drawer of his dresser. He'd given most of his wife's things to the Goodwill after she'd passed, but he couldn't part with her fancy towels. They could line his coffin with the things after he died.

He shuffled across the linoleum floor to the front door. Millie would have hated the floors. Would have covered them with throw rugs, but paint cleaned up easier off linoleum than carpet.

Robby stood in the hallway. Dark gray overcoat, collar turned up against the November cold. Salt and pepper hair that was still remarkably thick for a man only two years younger than Edgar.

Twenty years' worth of wrinkles cut creases in his old friend's forehead and cheeks. But Robby still had the same thick mustache that tickled the ladies when he kissed them on the cheek. The same scar along one side of his chin that he lied about whenever someone asked how he got it. And the same glint of mischief in his blue eyes as he looked up at Edgar, even if the blue had faded somewhat.

"You got old," Robby said in lieu of a greeting.

"Yeah, well there's a lot of that going around."

Edgar winced as soon as the words left his mouth. Not everybody got old.

Robby held up a brown paper bag. "I brought the good stuff. You got a couple of glasses in there?" He wrinkled his nose. "That don't have that paint goop in them?"

"I don't use glasses for that," Edgar said, but he stepped away from the door to let Robby in just the same.

He retrieved two mismatched water glasses from the kitchen. Millie would have been upset about that too, but most of the time he spent alone so who cared if his glasses matched?

He found Robby staring at the stack of canvasses leaning against one wall, probably two years' worth of Edgar's work.

"You've been keeping up," Robby said.

Edgar shrugged. "Keeps me busy."

Robby poured them each two fingers of bourbon. It went down smooth. Good stuff indeed.

They didn't toast to Mitch. They didn't have to. The booze was enough. The toast was implied.

"How was the funeral?" Edgar asked when the bourbon in his glass was almost gone along with most of the ache in his hands.

Robby shrugged. "It was a funeral. Prayers. Tears. Eulogies."

"You give one?"

"Hell, no." Robby reached for the bourbon and poured himself another finger. "What was I going to say? We pulled some jobs together? He was a great second-story man?"

Mitch had been more than that. He'd been an acrobat. Robby used to swear the man had no bones in his body, but of course, he had. In the end, those bones had done him in. His bones, and the bitch who'd turned on them all.

Edgar waved off the offer of a refill. The booze was just a stalling technique, a way for Robby to soften him up. That was the way he'd always operated. He'd come into your life out of the blue, soften you up, then tell you what he had in mind.

The hell of it was, he made you want it too. Even when you knew you shouldn't.

Edgar had been friends with Robby for more than half his life. He knew the man inside and out, the good and the bad.

He would have thought he'd know better by now, but he still felt the pull of those blue eyes and the force of the man's personality. Millie used to tell him that he loved Robby more than he loved her. Sitting here drinking with a man he hadn't seen in nearly two decades, he couldn't swear that she'd been wrong.

He put his glass down on the TV tray next to his palette. "I'm retired, you know."

Robby gave him a look that took Edgar back to those good old/bad old days. The look that said Robby wasn't buying anybody's bullshit.

"Guys like us never retire." Robby nodded at the paintings leaning against the wall. "You always were the best."

The best forger. The best copycat. Edgar had been working on leaving those skills behind. Developing his own style. His own art, not mimicking somebody else's.

"I'm retired," he said again.

Robby didn't say anything. He just sat in Edgar's best easy chair and stared at him with the same glint in his eye that he'd had when they'd both been young enough to pull off whatever Robby had in mind.

Edgar shifted in his seat. This chair had been Millie's, and it didn't quite fit his skinny ass. He'd gotten thinner with age while she'd grown softer, all the sharp edges gone.

It was no coincidence that it had taken Robby a week after Mitch's funeral to show up at Edgar's front door. If the visit was just to toast the memory of one of their own, he would have come sooner.

Robby was up to something. Planning things in that remarkable mind of his. The one that thought not one, not two, but a half dozen moves ahead. Edgar had learned early on not to play chess with the man. Chess or jobs, it was all a game to Robby, and games were made to be won.

They'd only lost once. Mitch had lost more than most of them, but they'd all lost.

Was that why he was here? To even the score?

Robby nodded as he watched the realization dawn on Edgar's face.

"You got a line on it," Edgar said.

"Right here in River City," Robby said.

"And it's doable?"

Of course, it was doable or Robby wouldn't be here.

He was going after the White Whale.

And he needed Edgar's help to pull it off.

———

THE JOB SHOULD HAVE BEEN a breeze. Would have been a breeze if Elise hadn't screwed them over.

Collectors paid Robby good money to go after objects no one else could obtain. Robby only took the jobs if they presented a challenge. It didn't matter what the object was. A sculpture. A painting. A priceless jewel or a hundred bars of gold in a hidden vault.

Robby could have been a decent second-story man himself, but where was the challenge in that? Simple thefts held no allure.

The White Whale wasn't a whale at all, but a priceless painting by the 16th Century Flemish artist Jan Brueghel the Elder. Priceless not only because of its age but because it was a previously unknown work. The collector had agreed to pay Robby five million upon delivery.

Elise thought they should ask for more.

She'd been their chameleon. Dress her down, and she could play the part of a blue-collar worker for the power company or the phone company or the cable company. Dress her up, put a few jewels around her neck and a few more dangling from her wrist, and she could pull off high society heiress worth a few million herself.

Her slight-of-hand was spectacular. Her fearlessness was unparalleled. She could walk into a den of vipers and come away unscathed.

It should have come as no surprise when she'd shot Mitch instead of giving him the painting. The painting had been hanging in a museum under heavy security—both human and electronic. The plan had been for Mitch to lower himself down from an overhead panel after Goldy, their tech guy, had disrupted the electronics and Elise had triggered the fire alarm, emptying the space of the high-dollar attendees at a special advance showing and the security guards hired to watch the painting and the attendees.

Mitch had set off the smoke bomb according to plan, lending credence to the fire alarm, but Elise hadn't left with the rest of the attendees. She was waiting for Mitch to remove the painting from the wall and take the canvas out of the frame, but she'd shot him before he got his part of the job done.

She'd shot him twice. Once in the shoulder, once in the hip.

She hadn't been aiming to kill him, only to disable him. She did a good job. The second shot shattered his pelvis. Mitch never walked right again.

She'd taken the original painting and used Mitch's escape route through the ceiling to disappear into the night. Rumor had it that she'd sold the painting for six million. Robby's team never saw a dime.

Mitch never turned on the team. He didn't even turn on Elise. He'd done the job in a black tux and slick black dress shoes. He claimed he was just another attendee and the smoke kept him from seeing who'd shot him.

He knew, though, and so did Robby.

Elise had ended Mitch's career. The painting became Robby's white whale. The one that got away. It stuck in his craw, but the painting had disappeared. So had Elise.

Until now.

"She's got it," Robby said.

Edgar sat in his apartment in Millie's favorite chair and sipped a second two fingers of the good bourbon Robby had brought.

"I thought she fenced it," Edgar said.

"She married the guy."

That made a kind of twisted sense. Why sell the painting to the collector and settle for six million when you can convince the guy to marry you so you can have access to the whole enchilada?

"It's been here all the time?" Edgar asked.

The aborted heist had been more than twenty-five years ago. The crew, minus Mitch and Elise, had done a couple of jobs since then, but the joy had gone out of it for Robby and eventually he quit putting new jobs together.

"Nah." Robby leaned back in his chair. "The guy's in high finance. Hedge funds. Shady stuff. Left the country when the feds started prosecuting his buddies. Now he's back. Guess he made friends in high places. Feels it's safe to show his face on this side of the world again."

"He brought it with him," Edgar said.

That made sense. Collectors kept their shit with them where they could see it, even if they were the only ones who ever would.

Edgar didn't have to ask why now.

It wasn't just for Mitch, but he was a big part of it. Mitch had been the youngest guy on the crew. Just young enough that he'd had a crush on Elise—pretty, sexy, treacherous Elise —and she'd shot him. That didn't sit well with Robby. It didn't sit well with Edgar either. None of them were getting any younger, and at their age, fate didn't present them with many opportunities to right the scales.

Righting the scales would be important to Robby.

To Edgar? Not so much. He'd figured out that life wasn't

fair after Millie had survived a bout with cancer only to be hit by a taxi two blocks from their apartment. She'd lingered on in the hospital for weeks. The insurance settlement had gone to pay her medical bills.

"You still got the fake you did back then?" Robby asked.

Elise hadn't taken the time to put the fake in the frame where the original had been. Edgar had been posing as another guest at the museum. He'd cut the fake out of the frame Mitch had dropped from the ceiling, rolled up the canvas, and walked out of the museum with the fake stashed under his raincoat.

"I painted over it," Edgar said. "Gave it to Mitch's kid's preschool."

Mitch's daughter had been three at the time, living with Mitch's ex. Edgar had painted a sunny scene of a park filled with jolly animals and laughing children over the fake Brueghel, put it in a cheap frame, and left it with the school's administrator. She'd told him she was sure the children would enjoy it.

Robby sat thinking for a minute before he nodded. "Can you do a second one?" he asked.

The White Whale had been a country setting with just enough religious idolatry thrown in to fit with Brueghel's classic style. Edgar was not only an extraordinary mimic when it came to art, he could remember every painting he'd ever copied. Even at his advanced age, he could remember the details of the Brueghel he'd copied all those years ago.

"Sure," he said. "Take me a week. Two if my arthritis kicks up, but sure. I can do it."

Two weeks would give Robby time to put the rest of a new crew together. Mitch hadn't been the only one of the old team who'd passed away, but he'd been the one who'd mattered the most. The one the rest of them had let down.

Edgar walked Robby to the door. Before he opened it, he looked Robby in those incredible blue eyes, dancing now again with the excitement of planning a heist.

"Last job," Edgar said. "I'm retired. I like my life."

Robby glanced away.

"That's got to be understood up front," Edgar said. "No more after this. I'm getting too old."

"Last job," Robby said. He wrinkled his nose in disgust. "How can you stand the smell of paint thinner?"

Edgar shrugged. "You get used to it. It wipes out a lot of mistakes."

Robby's voice was as flat as his expression, but he clapped Edgar on the shoulder. "We do this right, there won't be any mistakes."

Edgar stared at the closed door long after Robby left.

If they did this one right.

He must be out of his mind to even think about doing this. It must be the season. Millie had been the one who'd always made a big deal about Thanksgiving. Decorated their place for Christmas. This time of year, she was in his thoughts more often than not, and he missed her.

If she was here, she'd sit him down and tell him what he already knew.

The problem with white whales was that the whale always won. Even if Ahab killed his whale, in the end the whale always won.

———

THE ONLY MEMBER of the old crew Robby brought in was Digger. That wasn't the man's real name. He'd been in his late twenties back when the crew had done their last job, after Elise had disappeared into her new life. Bold and brash and a hell of a driver, Digger was down for doing anything that required any type of physical labor.

Like taking a sledgehammer to the interior walls of the penthouse next door to where Elise and her husband lived.

Robby had gotten his hands on a set of blueprints for the penthouse floor thanks to a bit of flirting with a city clerk nearing retirement age who'd been amazed that anyone like Robby would flirt with her. The penthouse floor had three apartments with a central elevator shaft. The blueprints didn't reflect any space in Elise's apartment that could be used as a safe room or a panic room.

Which meant that the Brueghel had to be hiding in plain sight. Behind a sliding panel installed after the basic space had been built out. Or nestled behind a larger painting that no doubt was wired to a security system. Or hell, even hung on a wall in her bedroom as a constant reminder of how she'd outsmarted Robby and the rest of them.

They couldn't go in through the ceiling, not even if they could find a second-story man with the acrobatic skill Mitch'd had. Elise had been in on that part of the original plan. She'd expect something like that. She probably had the air ducts and ceiling panels wired, with security cameras trained on every square inch of the apartment.

So Robby planned to go in through the front door.

Digger's job was to make as much noise as possible demolishing the walls next door. The place was empty, awaiting renovations that would start after the first of the year. Digger would just be giving the renovations an early start.

Elise's penthouse might be upscale with extra insulation in the walls, but a determined man wielding a sledgehammer and listening to metal music at eardrum-shattering levels in the penthouse next door could make enough noise that Elise and her husband would think the guy was standing right next to them.

Digger started working with the sledgehammer and metal music a week before the heist was scheduled to go down. Robby figured that after a week of listening to all the pounding and screaming, Elise's nerves, not to mention her husband's, would be shot. It helped that her husband appeared to do most of his work from a small corner office in the penthouse, so it wasn't like he could escape to an outside office.

That's when Chester would come in. Chester was their new

chameleon, only unlike Elise who'd used her beauty to blend in, Chester was so unremarkable, so every day, he became totally forgettable. Have a police sketch artist try to draw his picture, and the result would look like any one of a thousand other middle-aged guys on the street. Put a pair of glasses on him, and he looked like an accountant. Put him in a hard hat with a pencil stuck behind one ear, and he looked like a contractor. Give him a clipboard, and he looked like a city inspector.

That was his job here. Fire inspector. He would be going through Elise's apartment and checking the alarms in each room to make sure they all worked—more noise to frazzle their nerves—and that the fire suppression system was in working order. In reality, he'd be looking for the Brueghel, or a reasonable place where the Brueghel might be hidden.

The crew's new tech guy was the grandson of their original tech guy. Goldy had passed away in front of his computer, hands on the keys, while he was in the middle of coding a new program that did things Edgar couldn't hope to understand. His grandson, who went by the handle Space-Case214, not only finished writing the program, he sold it to some guys in Silicon Valley for cash up front and a piece of the gross, not the profits.

At nineteen, SpaceCase was not only independently wealthy, Robby said he was the smartest tech geek he'd ever met. Even better than Goldy.

"Covers his tracks like you wouldn't believe," he'd said. "He could make either of us disappear like that," and he snapped his fingers.

Not literally. SpaceCase didn't have a violent bone in his

body. He did, however, hold some sort of record on the dark web for making the most information disappear in a single hour. Probably less than an hour.

His job was to redirect Elise's home security feeds and replace them with dummy feeds.

"He told me he could have done that when he was a kid," Robby said.

Like he was all that much older now. Edgar had met the kid only once, and he made Edgar feel like he should be in an old folks' home gumming his oatmeal.

The actual robbery would be handled by their new second-story man, who happened to be a woman. Rory was thin and lithe and contorted herself into yoga positions that made Edgar's joints hurt just thinking about them. She could crack a safe, pick a lock, or take the watch off your wrist while you had your eyes on your hand the whole time.

This time around Edgar had painted the fake Brueghel on an oversized canvas, then cut the painting out after the oil had dried. It wouldn't stand up to an insurance inspection—pigments had changed over the centuries—but it didn't have to. It wasn't like Elise would ever insure a stolen treasure like the Brueghel. All it had to do was fool Elise and her husband long enough that they wouldn't be able to trace the theft back to any of Robby's crew.

Chester the fire inspector would find something wrong with the fire suppression system in Elise's penthouse. He'd come back with Rory, disguised as a tech for the contractor who'd installed the suppression system. Accompanying Rory would be the team's last member, a muscle-bound weightlifter named Roscoe. His job was to haul around the suppression system's replacement cannisters.

Inside one of those cannisters would be Edgar's fake Brueghel.

On a signal from Rory, SpaceCase would cut into the apartment's security feeds. He'd also send a signal to Digger, who would punch a hole through the connecting wall between the two apartments.

While Elise and her husband, annoyed now beyond reason, went to chew out Digger, Rory would liberate the Brueghel from its frame and replace it with Edgar's forgery. He'd shown her how to do a quick and dirty job that would be enough to get the team out of the apartment with the real painting safely enclosed in the dummy cannister.

Or at least that's the way it should have worked.

During his first visit, Chester had identified two potential spots where Elise might have hidden the Brueghel—one behind another painting in an interior room with an antique billiards table and a wet bar, and one behind a gilded accent piece suspended from the ceiling that took up half a wall in the bedroom. Chester's description had been "a gold-plated piece of lattice" surrounded by light fixtures that made it impossible to see more than shadows behind the fixture.

"It looks like the whole thing might slide out of the way," he'd told Robby. "My money's on that."

The first part of the heist had gone smooth as silk. Rory and Roscoe got into the apartment, lugging the cannisters on a dolly. Once inside, they'd sent the signal to SpaceCase. He'd disrupted the apartment's security and sent the signal to Digger.

Right on time, Digger had broken through the adjoining wall between the two penthouses at a spot that put the hole in Elise's living room, far enough away from the bedroom to give Rory and Roscoe time to work.

The plan went south when instead of confronting an angry Elise, Digger found himself staring at the business end of her gun.

"Get ahold of Robby," she told Digger. "I want to say hello."

EDGAR, Robby, and SpaceCase had been watching the whole heist go down on a series of monitors in a utility van parked half a block away from Elise's apartment. SpaceCase had equipped Digger's hard hat, along with the nametags Rory and Roscoe wore, with miniature cameras and microphones that he said were state of the art.

Until Elise pulled the gun on Digger, Edgar had been feeling pretty good about the plan.

He should have known better. Elise was many things, but she wasn't stupid.

"Oh, shit," SpaceCase said as Elise's image filled the entire screen that displayed Digger's feed. "I don't do guns, guys. She fires that thing, I'm outta here."

Edgar swore under his breath. He'd seen the aftermath when she'd shot Mitch, but he hadn't seen her actually pull the trigger. He didn't want to see her pull the trigger now.

"He's watching," Digger told Elise, his voice remarkably calm.

Elise told Digger to turn the music off. The view on the monitor swung crazily around the penthouse where Digger had been working, and the metal music switched off. For the first time, Edgar could hear the soft Christmas music playing in the background in Elise's living room.

On the other two monitors, Edgar watched helplessly as Elise's husband rounded up Rory and Roscoe, also at gunpoint. The gun he held was bigger than the one Elise had. Apparently former hedge fund managers didn't rely solely on bodyguards to protect themselves.

Digger's camera swung back to face Elise. Over her shoulder, an icy white Christmas tree trimmed in gold stood in sharp contrast to the cold steel of her gun.

"You always were too smart for your own good," she said, clearly talking to Robby, not Digger. "You should have used all new people. I had an idea who was behind all the racket once I caught Digger getting out of the elevator one night."

Her gaze flickered to Digger's face. "You've aged pretty well, I have to admit."

Robby leaned forward so that he could talk into the

microphone that sent a signal to the earpieces the team wore. The earpieces looked like wireless earbuds, the same thing Edgar saw twenty times a day walking down to the grocery store.

"Let me talk to her," Robby told Digger.

The monitor showed Digger holding out his earpiece to Elise. She took it, and now when she spoke, her voice echoed. SpaceCase fiddled with something on his keyboard and the echoes died away.

"I didn't think you'd remember him," Robby said to Elise. "He wasn't really on your radar. Not like Mitch."

One side of her mouth twitched, but that was the only reaction to the mention of Mitch's name.

"Edgar there with you too?" she asked. "If we open one of those cannisters, will we find his work there?"

"Some of it," Robby admitted. "He's gotten pretty good. You should see his stuff. It's hanging all over town."

"Good for him."

Elise's mouth thinned down to a hard line. She hadn't aged all that well herself. The micro camera wasn't good enough to show any fine lines around her eyes, but her mouth was bracketed by the kind of wrinkles women got when they spent their lives disapproving of everything around them.

Or maybe spent their lives looking over their shoulders, waiting for old debts to come due.

"So you got me," Robby said.

"Again," Elise said.

"Again," Robby agreed.

Edgar gave him a sideways glance. Robby was taking this

far better than Edgar expected. Maybe the intervening years had mellowed him.

Maybe he'd decided he didn't want to be Ahab after all.

"What say we call this a draw," Robby said. "Everybody walk away."

Elise cocked her head to one side. "The great Robby Chase, admitting defeat?" She snorted, an unladylike sound. "I knew you were getting old. I didn't know you'd gone senile."

"No need to get nasty," Robby said. "You've still got your prize. Still pulled one over on me." He shrugged, even though Elise couldn't see it. "Had to give it a shot for Mitch."

Her mouth twitched again.

Robby must have caught it. He leaned closer to the microphone and lowered his voice. "You owe me one for that," he said. "Pay up."

That got to her. Edgar could see it. She glanced away from Digger. It was long enough that Digger could have tried to take the gun away from her, but he stood still. He hadn't been in on the conversation since he'd given his earpiece away.

Elise turned back toward Digger, but her eyes were focused on the camera. She must have known exactly where it was imbedded in Digger's hardhat. She always had been a smart woman. Devious and deceitful, but smart.

"Get your crew out of here," she said. "I see any of you again, I won't be so forgiving."

She gestured with the gun. Digger didn't have to be told twice. Neither did Rory and Roscoe. Digger bent to gather up his tools, which gave everyone in the utility van a perfect shot of the mess he'd made in the adjoining penthouse.

What they didn't get was a shot of Elise's face when Robby got in the last word before he killed his microphone.

"Don't worry about seeing me again," Robby told her. "This was my last job. I'm retired."

ROBBY PAID the crew for their time and effort before he told them goodbye. "I'm taking a page out of Edgar's book," he said. "I would have liked to go out with a win, but a draw's better than dead."

As final toasts went, it wasn't half bad.

They'd all met in the back room of an Italian restaurant that had been a favorite of Robby's back in the day. The place had been decorated for the holidays with a real Christmas tree and poinsettias and strings of lights with large multicolor bulbs, the kind Edgar remembered from when he'd been a kid. The sound system featured Sinatra and Martin and Bennett crooning carols from the '50s with an occasional Bing Crosby thrown in for good measure, and the candles in all the old Chianti bottles that served as candleholders on the tables were all red or green.

The place reminded Edgar of Christmases with Millie. They'd never had a tree, their apartments had been too small, but as for the rest of it? She'd done it up right. She hadn't even minded when Robby invited himself over for Christmas dinner.

The crew ate too much, drank too much red wine—far too much for someone SpaceCase's age—and when the meal was over, they all wandered off one by one to go their separate ways.

Edgar and Robby were the last to leave. They stood on the cracked sidewalk in front of the restaurant, bundled up in long overcoats against the cold. The weather had turned nasty two days after the aborted job, slushy snow blanketing the city. The snow had turned to ice in the deep shadows between the city's high rises, and the wind had a bite to it that promised even more snow for the last few days before Christmas. Fitting for December in the city.

Edgar decided to hail a cab, but Robby said he wanted to go for a walk.

"In this mess?" Edgar shook his head. "Old bones break easy, my friend."

Robby looked at him with that twinkle in his faded blue eyes. "I'm not worried about my bones," he said. "Old is old. Tonight made me feel young, but I don't think it's going to last."

Something in the way he said that last bit sent a chill down Edgar's spine that had nothing to do with the cold. "You got something you want to tell me?"

Robby clapped Edgar on the shoulder. "You've been a good friend to me, probably better than I deserved. I'm glad we did one more job together. For old time's sake."

Something was going on, but Edgar knew better than to push Robby about it. The man had his secrets. Everybody did.

Ever since his doctor had told him to cut out booze and cigarettes, Edgar had been donating his cigarette money to support scholarships at the high school Mitch's daughter had attended. He and Millie never had any kids of their own, and

Edgar had enough money to live on for however long he had left.

He'd never mentioned it to Mitch. The man had been too proud to accept any money from Edgar, and it was the best way Edgar could soothe his conscience. Elise could have shot him too in that smoke-filled exhibition room, left him alone and bleeding on the floor, but she hadn't. She'd only shot Mitch. Survivor's guilt was a bitch.

A cab pulled over. As Edgar opened the back door, he gave Robby as jaunty a wave as he could manage. His arthritis had come back, and even the wine hadn't helped.

Robby had touched two fingers to his head, then straightened his shoulders and turned his back on his old friend.

Edgar didn't know it at the time, but the sight of Robby Chase walking down the icy street, with his impossibly full head of salt and pepper hair and a charcoal gray knitted scarf wrapped around his neck, would be the last time he'd ever see his old friend.

Robby died after the turn of the new year.

Cancer.

Just like Mitch.

EDGAR LEARNED the rest of the story the day after Robby's funeral. A young woman delivered a plain manilla envelope to Edgar's apartment. He signed a messenger slip for it, then sat down in his comfortable chair to open it.

He recognized Robby's handwriting immediately.

His vision swam unexpectedly. He'd been fine at the

funeral, the only one of the old crew who'd attended. He hadn't given a eulogy. What could he say? Robby was one of the best heist men in the business? So he'd sat at the back of the funeral home, an old hat in his hands, and thought about how the twinkle had finally gone out of his friend's expressive blue eyes.

It took him longer than it should have to read what Robby had written. Any other man might have taken this information to the grave, but Robby had decided to share what he'd done with his oldest friend.

His best friend, as he'd written.

Robby had gotten the idea when Edgar had told him he'd painted over the initial fake Brueghel and given it to the preschool where Mitch's daughter had gone. Robby had contacted the daughter, grown now, and gotten the address.

The painting had still been there. Robby had offered the preschool an exorbitant sum to buy the painting. Always strapped for cash, the preschool had accepted.

Robby had taken the painting to another man he knew. Someone who restored old paintings and could be counted on to keep his mouth shut.

"Don't be shocked to learn you weren't my only painter," he'd written. "You're just the best."

The man had restored Edgar's original forgery. Robby had used that to replace the real Brueghel, which wasn't in Elise's penthouse apartment.

"The old man she married didn't trust her," Robby wrote. "Smart move since he knew she was a thief. So he had a fake made and hung that in their penthouse. From what I heard, his forger lives in Europe, so your reputation is intact. You're still the best in the states."

How Robby had managed to switch Edgar's restored fake with the real painting her husband had hidden or even where he'd hidden it, the letter didn't go into. Some secrets men took to their graves.

"I'm sending you a key inside a book," Robby wrote. "Media mail. It'll take a while to get there."

The key was to a locker at a local bus terminal. The original Brueghel was in the locker. The locker was paid up until the end of February.

"Keep it, return it, ignore it, it's up to you," Robby wrote. "You're my art guy. I trust you."

That had been the end of the letter. Robby hadn't signed it. He hadn't needed to. Simply writing the letter had been enough. The last job was finally done.

Edgar leaned back in his chair.

Robby had won.

He'd beaten Elise at her own game and she never knew it. Even if she eventually figured out the Brueghel in their apartment was a fake, she'd think her husband had stashed the original somewhere. He was a good fifteen years older than she was. She was banking on inheriting the real painting when he died.

Would she even think to check that her husband's "original" was real? Probably not. Not until she tried to fence it.

Edgar started to laugh. He laughed long enough and hard enough that tears streamed down his wrinkled face.

Robby had gone out in style, as only someone like Robby could.

Edgar got up and took Robby's handwritten pages to the kitchen. While the letter burned in his sink, he poured himself two fingers of the good stuff. Robby had left the bottle behind the last time he'd been there.

It should have been some kind of sign. Robby never left good booze behind.

He must have known he was dying the whole time he was planning the heists, both of them. Making one last run at his white whale.

Edgar didn't know what he'd do with the painting, but he had time to figure it out. He wasn't like Robby. He couldn't deal with fences, not anymore. His hands had been shaking the whole time he'd sat in the utility van while Elise held a gun on Digger.

He was retired. He intended to stay that way.

He raised his glass as the last of Robby's handwritten pages turned to ash. He'd wash the ashes down the drain, and then he'd go back to the painting he'd been working on. A portrait of Millie as she'd looked on their wedding day, young and radiant in a gown whiter than the January snow falling outside his window.

"Here's to you, Robby," he said. "You did it, my friend. You actually did it."

He'd finally beaten his white whale.

START HERE

DivingintotheWreck.com

KRISTINE KATHRYN RUSCH

Kristine Kathryn Rusch is a New York Times *and* USA Today *bestselling writer and maybe the most award-winning and prolific writer working today. She has won more awards in science fiction and mystery than just about anyone alive and she is the only person to win the Hugo Award for her writing as well as her editing.*

Since this issue has a lot of stories that will twist at you by the end, I thought I would end the issue with one of Kris's best-known novellas that has the same feeling.

You can find out a lot more about Kris's work at her publisher, WMG Publishing Inc www.wmgbooks.com *or her website* www.kriswrites.com

SEPTEMBER AT WALL AND BROAD

KRISTINE KATHRYN RUSCH

Manhattan

September 16, 1920

SHE DIDN'T WANT to go to work this morning. Normally, Philippa couldn't wait to leave the tiny two-room walkup she shared with five other women. The place smelled of grease and dirt so old that no amount of bleach would get it out. She had tried to clean the flat when she realized she would have to live like everyone else in this godforsaken century. She scrubbed the place until her hands were raw, and made no difference whatsoever.

Ambition was cold comfort when you shared a mattress with two other women—girls in 1920 parlance—neither of whom had bathed in the last week. The flat had two windows, both of which overlooked the brick building next door. No breezes, no sunlight.

Not that it mattered. She stayed out of the flat as much as

she could, coming back to sleep and change clothes. She probably smelled no better than her companions. The bathroom was down the hall, the bathtub foul, and the toilet an atrocity.

She'd been counting the days to September 16, not because that was the day she'd been waiting for, but because she'd be able to go home, real home, bathe, sleep in a bed with Egyptian cotton sheets, and turn on the air conditioning, even if she didn't need it.

For the first time in her entire career, she missed the middle of the 21st century. She missed it with a mad passion, realizing that with all the rising sea levels, the incredible population growth, the poverty that no one could quite wipe out, the life she led there was one of privilege, even though she associated more with the upper class here than she ever had there.

Still, she stood at the door of her apartment building, and looked up at the azure sky. A perfect blue, the temperature in the low sixties, promising to be one of those spectacular New York days, the kind that made you wonder why you lived anywhere else. The city, about to enter its ascendancy in American life, glowed under the September sun.

People were walking outside and gazing upward, some even smiling, probably planning a series of errands that would get them out of the office. Folks who worked outside had smirks of superiority; they got paid to be outside.

A few people were probably thinking ahead to lunch, planning to splurge at one of the food carts, and maybe even sit on one of the benches lined up along the streets or head to one of the city's parks, if only for a few minutes. A few snatched minutes that no one would ever get.

She shuddered. She'd been in Manhattan before on a perfect September day. On one of her first jobs, in fact. She'd stood not far from here and gazed upward at a building that wasn't even a glimmer in someone's eye this morning, and watched, at 8:46 am, as American Flight 11 crashed into the World Trade Center's north tower.

The same sort of sunshine. Same kind of optimism in the air.

Only then that crisis had been more deadly, using weapons not yet dreamed of, hitting a building impossible to build in this time period, while an entire nation watched on a machine that Philo Farnsworth wouldn't even imagine for another year.

That day had been hard, but she had been prepared. She had watched the footage, read the accounts, talked to others who had also visited September 11th. And that day had been the final test in her training: could she maintain her composure as people jumped to their deaths to escape flames, as buildings pancaked around her, as first responders who wouldn't live out the day ran past her to save as many lives as possible?

She had been, in the words of her instructor, "positively bloodless." He had meant that as a compliment, and she had taken it that way. "Positively bloodless," meant she kept her composure, did her job, and got out with a minimum of notification and a minimum of fuss.

Yes, she had nightmares. Everyone did; it was part of the job. But they weren't debilitating, and she was able to work through the worst of them with the therapist the department had assigned her.

She was, in other words, a stellar candidate, the best of her class. A woman who had since completed dozens of difficult assignments.

A woman who did not want to walk to the corner of Wall and Broad on this beautiful September morning. A woman who did not want to enter the House of Morgan to take her lowly secretary's desk with its fancy expensive Underwood typewriter, something she had been instructed to be very, very careful with because it was delicate. It wasn't delicate. The damn thing was a tank and it would take a sledgehammer to destroy it.

She would wager, if she had anyone to wager with, that the Underwood would survive today's bombing with nary a scratch.

She sighed, and stepped into the sea of humanity. Only four hours left, and she needed to make the most of them.

———

Washington, D.C.
March 23, 2057 (Supposedly)

ASSISTANT ATTORNEY GENERAL Preston Lane needed a moment to process the information the four people behind him had just presented.

He pivoted and faced the floor-to-ceiling window of his office in the Time Department's building. The building was known as the Bubble for a variety of reasons. The first was obvious: its round glass shape looked like a bubble. But the second was because it was protected by time bubble after time bubble after time bubble. "Time bubbles" were the nick-name for "time-guards." In some ways, time bubble was more accurate, in that the bubble froze a time period into place.

He worked here instead of the Robert F. Kennedy Depart-ment of Justice building (which was a nice, but old building) because the Time Division of the Justice Department, like all time-related government departments, had offices here. The Bubble protected all who served.

The yard outside was in full spring bloom. Cherry trees lined the wall, their blossoms in full pink flower. The green grass, the emerging foliage, all spoke of a fantastic DC spring.

Which hadn't quite arrived in DC yet.

The permanent staff blew smoke up his ass about the yard. *It's enclosed, so it follows its own schedule,* the head gardener told him when he'd asked. *Think of it like a greenhouse.*

A greenhouse with a manipulated timer. He'd gone into the archives shortly after receiving his assignment and looked. This year's cherry blossoms mimicked last year's weather. Last year, the trees had reached full bloom by the end of March, just like they had for the past thirty years. This year, the trees outside the Bubble had returned to their April schedule, the one that had made this city and its cherry trees justly famous.

Plants didn't cooperate inside a time bubble. If you wanted plants to bloom and grow, they actually needed care, just like they would in a greenhouse. If you wanted to pretend that they followed the same schedule as the outside world, you didn't speed up the timeline or import different plants from different time periods. You set the yard's chronometer to its own schedule, and prayed that it worked like the rest of the world.

Which it did not. The world was/is/will always be a messy place. For the plants inside the yard, the world had an unbreakable schedule, and theoretically, the entire staff enjoyed that.

It made his skin crawl. All of this did. The deeper he got into his assignment, the more unhappy he became.

Especially with the Wall Street case.

Before he got appointed to the Time Division, someone on staff had noticed that Manhattan's financial district had been time-guarded from mid-August to mid-September 1920. Time-guards in the United States needed approval from the Time Department. The Secretary of Time had claimed she knew nothing of this, and indeed, there were no records of who or what had installed that bubble.

Plus, the bubble did not conform to government regulations.

Government-formed time bubbles existed throughout the United State's history, and they also existed now. The White House had its own time bubble, as did Congress, the Supreme Court, and the Pentagon. All of the buildings housing the Cabinet had them as well. Not every place could be protected —if someone could easily get to a United States Representative, for example, because the country did not have enough money to protect district offices. The money instead went to time-guarding polling places on each and every election day in the country, no matter how small the election.

Lane did not have the ability to reset time. Officially, no

one did. But he suspected someone held that power unofficially, and that someone or those someones existed in the very government he served.

But the answer to that question was above his pay grade.

What happened to Philippa D'Arco, however, was not.

Lane took a deep breath. He'd go out into the yard and walk among the cherry blossoms if he weren't allergic to the damn things. Because he needed to move.

But he couldn't, because he had to finish this meeting. He turned his back on the windows. Wilhelmina Rutger and her three assistants still stood behind him, ignoring the comfortable chairs and the hollow tables that allowed for some selected time viewing.

His wife would be furious. He was supposed to accompany her on some important dinner for her hedge-fund business. She had probably given up on him anyway. She didn't understand the government's mandate: anyone who worked in the Bubble had to take a second oath, vowing to never ever use time travel for personal gain.

Even if that gain was keeping peace in a marriage already on the rocks.

He forced his attention back to the problem at hand—not his problem, but the division's problem. They were related, after all.

"Okay, let me see if I get this straight." He had started so many conversations like this in the six months since his appointment. Time travel's complexities made his brain hurt. "D'Arco had ten windows for return and missed all of them, which is, apparently, unlike her. She's also the first investigator we've sent to the September 16th bombing who failed to return."

"Yes." Wilhelmina was petite and blond, with a friendly face completely at odds with her take-no-prisoners personality. "Philippa's body didn't return either, which is our failsafe."

Wilhelmina peered at him, as if she were testing whether or not he actually knew that. He wasn't sure he did. He tried not to look even more creeped out. He hated the way that people just vanished when they stepped into the time chamber, even if the vanishing was only for a moment or two. He didn't want to think about how he'd feel if they came back a few seconds later as a corpse.

"In other words this is extremely unusual." Lane sighed again, and swept his hand at the chairs. "Let's sit."

They did. He frowned at the assistants, having no idea who they were. Wilhelmina always seemed to bring a different set of assistants to every meeting. Lane wasn't sure if that was because she couldn't keep assistants or if her assistants swapped out due to those time complexities.

"Philippa is the first woman we've sent to the Wall Street

bombing," Wilhelmina said. "Our previous investigators were all men. The first one arrived just after the time bubble burst, 12:01 pm on September 16, 1920, one minute after the bomb went off. He couldn't even get into the bomb site at Wall and Broad. We tried to have our second investigator arrive at 12:02 pm, and he couldn't do that. He could travel outside the time bubble around the financial district, but he couldn't time-travel inside it within hours of that explosion. We sent our third investigator to Manhattan one month before the explosion with the idea that he would get a job that would allow him to investigate the entire area, and see if the historical record is missing something that we should know."

Lane remembered now. "That last guy is the reason we ended up sending Philippa."

"Yes." Wilhelmina smiled, even though the smile did not go to her eyes. The smile said, *We've had this conversation and you should remember it. All of it. I hate repeating myself. Sir.*

He did remember the conversation now. He had asked her, *Why weren't we aware of the rigid class structure in New York at that time?*

It's not class structure that we're running into per se, sir, Wilhelmina had told him. *It's nepotism. To get hired in the House of Morgan, you need to have some kind of relationship with someone who does work there. And in 1920, we're at the height of the corruption that became known as the Teapot Dome Scandal. Everyone inside the New York Police Department who could hire our man won't now, because he has no ties to Tammany Hall. We—*

He'd cut her off. He had no idea what Teapot Dome was, and didn't want to find out. The same with Tammany Hall. He had some historical expertise, but it wasn't New York in the

1920s. When he accepted the President's appointment as Head of the Time Division in the Attorney General's Office, Lane had hoped to use this job to deal with interesting things, like people traveling back in time to murder someone else's grandmother who just happened to be a federal judge or something.

Instead, he was dealing with protected time periods that hadn't been protected by the proper authorities, and hints and allegations of alleged time abuse. Half his staff was somewhen else at the moment, investigating, prodding, poking, seeing there was a case. Or, as his boss, the Attorney General, liked to say when he brought potential cases to her, the staff was seeing if this was something that would "benefit us in the next election, or is it something that we can leave on the scrapheap of history for the next administration?"

Maybe he should quit, before the cynicism took him out of the game entirely.

"Sir?" Wilhelmina asked.

He'd checked out again. He wondered if he could pretend it was because he didn't understand the time paradoxes.

"No one looked at young women in that period," Wilhelmina said through gritted teeth. She was clearly repeating herself. "If they had jobs, they were clearly from the wrong class and being women, they were considered stupid."

He had no idea how anyone could find women stupid. There had to have been women like Wilhelmina in that day and age. How had anyone believed they were inferior?

"Philippa is one of our best operatives," Wilhelmina said. "She studied the bombing for three months before we sent her back. She's spent a month In Time."

Lane hated that phrase. It came from In Country, military slang for foreign territory, particularly a war zone. But its use here often confused him, because the rest of the world always wanted him to do things "in time" as well, and it meant something completely different. Like "just in the nick of time," which was the only way he'd make that dinner date now.

"Philippa couldn't have been killed in the bombing. She knew where she should stand, what she should do, where the most victims were, the greatest danger. She knew it all. She also knew she could return to us at 12:01, and give us her information. She would have come back, sir. I know it."

Wilhelmina's voice shook as she said that last, not with anger, but with sorrow. Or was it fear? Either way, he'd never heard those two emotions in her voice. Now she had his full attention.

"So what do you want to do?" he asked.

Wilhelmina was authorized to do a lot on her own. The fact that she had come here, with a request that she hadn't yet articulated, meant something was very different.

"I want to send in an investigator, sir," Wilhelmina said.

He frowned. "We already sent in three, not counting Philippa. At a certain point, we have to decide that we have done what we can on this investigation. We only have so many resources."

"We don't leave people in the field," one of the men snapped. Everyone looked at him. He paled. "Sir. Sorry, sir. I mean, after all. She could be in trouble."

Could have been *in trouble,* Lane mentally corrected. But he didn't say it. He continued to address his questions to

Wilhelmina. "Do we have information on her after September 16?"

"In a cursory search of the historical record, her alias, which is Philippa Darcy, does not show up. But it doesn't mean anything. Thirty-eight people died that day, and 143 were seriously wounded. But that was according to the statistics released long after the fact. No one put up flyers or tracked everyone who had been on the street that day. Even if they had the resources, they didn't have the will. The newspaper reports, for godssake, only listed names and address of the lower-class victims, and that was only if they got identified. The authorities didn't even know for certain if the body parts they found matched up to the—"

"I'm aware of the vagaries of the pre-technological age of investigation," Lane said. "I'm asking if Philippa Darcy married or showed up in the public records. Maybe she had done her best to leave a message…?"

The investigators were supposed to send their recall device back if, for some odd reason, they decided to stay in the past. Only a handful of people had ever stayed, and all of those had traveled back just a few years, not more than a century.

"No message, sir," Wilhelmina said. "We checked. But Philippa is in the payroll roster in the House of Morgan for the week before. There is no payroll roster for the week of the 16th, and she isn't on it the following week."

Lane placed his hands on his knees and slid back. "Clearly there's a problem with the time-guard around that time period. What we've been doing hasn't been working, so I don't think sending another investigator into that time-guarded period is the best answer. I think you'll need to come up with a new plan to figure out how this bubble got placed, and who placed it."

One of her assistants slumped, but Wilhelmina's back straightened.

"I'm not asking for someone new to investigate the bombing or that time-guard, sir," she said in a how-dumb-are-you voice. "I'm asking to send an investigator to locate Philippa. I have to believe that she knows something, that she discovered something, and that someone is preventing her return. None of our failsafes have worked, and at least one of them should have. We should have some knowledge of what happened to her, and we have none."

"You automatically leap from this mission didn't go right to someone has harmed her?" It was Lane's turn to use the how-dumb-are-you voice. "For all we know, she could have been standing too close to the bomb when it went off, and she got vaporized. She, her device, the failsafes, everything. After all, as you just pointed out, our information from that time period isn't exactly trustworthy. And I seem to recall that they never did figure out with any certainty what happened that day."

The third assistant grimaced. "There's a lot of evidence to suggest—"

Wilhelmina held up a hand, silencing him. "We do an out-and-back," she said. "A short mission, looking only on that day. We send in someone new.

We give him the right credentials.

After all, William J. Flynn took a train in from DC the

moment he heard about the bombing. We can have our man take jurisdiction for just a few hours."

Lane had no idea who this William J. Flynn was, although he supposed Wilhelmina had once briefed him on that as well. So many cases, so much to remember. Maybe he would resign at the end of the year. Clearly all of these time paradoxes were taking a toll.

"I thought we already did that," Lane said. "Wasn't that our second investigator?"

She glanced at her assistants. "We had the wrong credentials."

"What?" Lane asked. He knew he hadn't heard this.

"We had legitimate New York police department credentials, but we had given our man a position too high up in the department. They figured out fairly quickly that he was a fraud. Only they figured he worked for former Commissioner Arthur Woods, not that he had come from the future."

Arthur Woods. Another name Lane probably should have remembered. He sighed. He would have to read up on this entire investigation just to refresh his memory.

He could either do that, or trust the woman who sat before him.

"How much will this cost the department?" Lane asked.

"It depends," she said flatly. "You can calculate the loss of a human life and the loss of the training we invested into the investigator, or you can figure the price of one more trip into time."

"Possibly losing another investigator," he said.

"Possibly," she said.

"If we do, we both lose our jobs," he said.

"*That's* what's worrying you?" she asked.

"No," he said. "It isn't. What worries me is that we're doing something we don't entirely understand. We're throwing more resources at it rather than investigating the best methods and then taking them. There is no hurry, Ms. Rutger, as you've often told me. If we send in someone today or next week, it won't matter. They'll still go back to the same time period."

She raised her chin ever so slightly. He had gotten through.

"You're right, of course," she said. "In my concern, I had forgotten that. We will conduct a more thorough investigation, and then I will consult with you again."

"Thank you," he said.

Wilhelmina and her assistants left, but he remained seated. Something about this disturbed him greatly. Not Wilhelmina's hurry or even the assistants' passion. In fact, he understood the assistants' passion. They could have been the ones on the front lines. But for the luck of the draw, this conversation could have been about any one of them.

No, something else bothered Lane.

New York's financial district. Three major attacks that he knew of: this one in 1920, the 1993 bombing of the World Trade Center, and the 2001 destruction of the World Trade Center. Plus at least two thwarted attacks, one in 2012 against the Federal Reserve in lower Manhattan, and another in 2025 against the New York Stock Exchange.

Were they all time-guarded events? If so, were they time-guarded by Homeland or Justice or the Time Department? Or by someone else? Something else? A multinational? A foreign government?

Lane stood up slowly. He had to make a choice here. He could remain the ignorant figurehead, disappointed in the job that they had given him, or he could step into his role as the chief investigator of time irregularities for the Federal Government.

He hated those dinners his wife planned. He used to love investigative work. He'd simply been overwhelmed by his learning curve and, if he were honest, by the fact that he walked through several time bubbles every morning when he came to work. He hated the Bubble, but everywhere he'd worked in DC had a time-guard of one type or another. The problem wasn't the job; the problem was his attitude.

He'd allowed others to dictate policy during his first six months here. Time to change that, no pun intended. Or maybe he did intend to pun. Because it was past time. And he couldn't use the amazing resources at his disposal to start again. So maybe he could use them to solve something huge.

Or, if this wasn't huge, just to make the right decision in the Philippa D'Arcy case.

Whatever that decision might be.

Manhattan
September 16, 1920

PHILIPPA GLANCED AT the clock hanging on the far wall. The incredible clack of typewriters had its own rhythm, a *rat-a-tat-tat-tat-tat-tat-tat bing!* that had become familiar to her. At the desk next to her, the new hire sang "Over There" faintly under her breath, a reprieve from the Tin Pan Alley tunes she had started the morning with. The last few hours of Philippa's last day. She looked at all the girls around her, intent on their typing or fixing their shorthand or stacking already-completed letters in manila folders, and wondered how they would fare.

They might be all right. The large room had no windows, the grillwork making it seem like a prison. All of the girls who worked there wore white shirtwaists and long skirts, their hair in a neat bun. They seemed interchangeable and probably were, to the men who ran the House of Morgan.

Philippa straightened her desk, rolled a sheet of House of Morgan letterhead in the platen of her Underwood, and stood up.

Mrs. Fontaine looked up from her desk. It faced the rows and rows of desks.

"You do not have permission to stand," she said. She was twice the age of the girls and twice their weight. She ran a tight office, but a fair one. She pretended to be an ogre, but the girls loved her, because she understood what it was to be young and employed and a little bit terrified.

"I'm sorry," Philippa said. "I'm afraid I need a personal moment."

Technically, the girls weren't to leave their desks until their thirty minute unpaid lunch break. But Mrs. Fontaine understood that women couldn't always sit that long, particularly at certain times of the month. She claimed she got her girls to do five times the work the girls in other financial houses did, because she allowed them "personal moments."

Mrs. Fontaine nodded. "Make it quick."

Philippa wouldn't make it quick. Not that it mattered. After noon today, she would no longer be employed at the House of Morgan.

She would make one more tour around the building, and try to see if there was something unusual. Then she would return to her desk and prevent some of the girls whom she'd befriended from taking their usual lunch. They would be safe inside their windowless room, but on that street, near the Curb Market, the Sub-Treasury, the New York Stock Exchange annex, and all of the other buildings, people would die, lose limbs, have their lives forever changed.

Technically, she wasn't supposed to prevent that. Technically, she was supposed to go about her business. But there was no way of knowing what the girls would have done without her, so trying to play that game didn't work. She had to live with herself, and even though, in her real life, in her real time, these women were long dead, they were alive now, she'd been their friend, and she owed them.

She slipped a steno pad into the pocket of her long skirt,

and stepped away from her desk. She smiled a thank you to Mrs. Fontaine, then headed in the direction of the women's necessary. The one great thing about the House of Morgan was that it had bathrooms and they were clean. Not that she needed to use one.

She waited until she was out of Mrs. Fontaine's sight, then pulled the steno pad from the pocket of her skirt. She hugged the pad against her chest and then wandered, making certain she looked lost.

It had worked every time she had done this in the past. Some man would ask her where she needed to go, she would give an answer, and he would point her in the right direction. The younger men would ask her name, and give her a bright smile. The older men would sometimes put their arm around her and guide her to the correct floor.

She didn't want either to happen today. She needed to do her last tour unescorted. Then, if she didn't find anything, she would slip onto the street and run to the Sub-Treasury building.

She couldn't get their mission off her mind either. Right now, as she patrolled the inside of the House of Morgan, workers at the Sub-Treasury building were transferring a billion dollars in gold coins and bullion to the federal assay office across the street.

She had no real idea how they were doing this; her reading told her that the workers were using a wooden chute, and after the bombing, a U.S. Army battalion would arrive to protect the gold.

Initially the Time Crimes Division believed someone was trying to steal the gold. After the first investigator discovered that no gold got stolen, someone suggested that the time-guard had been put into place to *prevent* the gold from getting stolen, and had been successful.

But that didn't make sense either, because the gold would be a lot easier to steal after the bombing than before. Hell, she could figure out how to do it: she could time travel into the Sub-Treasury or next to the chute in the assay office at 12:01 in the chaos. With the right kind of manpower and weaponry, the gold would disappear.

But it didn't; it wouldn't; it never would. It would remain.

The fact that she was even thinking of heading to the Sub-Treasury building showed just how desperate she was to get some information, any information, before she left 1920 at 12:02 pm. She had already been to Sub-Treasury courtesy of a nice young guard, who had thought her harmless. A different nice young guard had shown her what he could in the assay office, and there, she found nothing out of the ordinary.

Not that she knew what she was looking for. Something. Something had to be here, besides this bombing.

Something had to be so important that changing it threatened The Way Things Were.

She walked up a marble staircase to the private meetings floor. She'd been called into a few of these conference rooms. She'd sat on a wooden chair in the back and taken notes.

Today, if someone asked where she was going, she had a half-plausible lie based on that previous experience. She knew that Junius Spencer Morgan the younger, the heir to the throne, was having a meeting in one of the rooms facing Wall Street. She'd seen photographs of the aftermath, although she wasn't sure which room he was in. If someone stopped her, she would tell them she was going to relieve the secretary handling that meeting.

But no one stopped her. She went up staircase after staircase to floor after floor and she was about to give up, when she noticed one of the doors to the maintenance area stood open.

She'd tried that door in the past, and it had been locked. This time, she slipped inside.

Four men were leaning together, gesturing and whispering. They appeared to be arguing. They didn't notice her.

They didn't look like maintenance men. They were too clean for one thing. People who did physical labor in this decade had a layer of grime on their clothes and skin that just couldn't come off in a weekly bath. Their clothes were off too. A little too shiny, a bit too new. And one man wore shoes that had a metal ridge she had never seen before. Or, rather, that she hadn't seen in a very long time. Or, rather, that no one would see for many many years.

The men all looked at her at the same time. One man flushed red.

"Can we help you?" asked the man wearing the odd shoes. He had dark eyes and skin that wasn't quite white. She wouldn't have noticed that a month ago, but after living here, in a world where everything was defined by skin color, last name, education, and accent, she noticed.

Her heart started pounding. Her planned lie about Mr. Morgan seemed wrong, somehow.

"I saw the open door..." she said.

"Christ," hissed the man who flushed. "She saw us. No one was supposed to see us."

His teeth were white. Even. Perfect. So were the teeth of the first man who spoke. So were her teeth. People here remarked on that.

These men didn't belong here any more than she did. And, she would wager, no one in the Time Division knew about them.

She backed out of the room, slammed the door closed, and ran for the stairs. With one hand, she lifted her skirt enough so that her own boots didn't catch, and with the other, she put the steno pad in her pocket. Then she reached for the railing. The steps were slick, and she had to slow down some.

She heard footsteps behind her. She sped up just as someone grabbed her. He smelled of cologne. Not Bay Rum. Cologne. Nothing from this time period. It was too subtle, too complex. And the hand that covered her mouth had had a manicure.

She bit his palm. He cursed, but didn't let her go. Instead, he dragged her up the stairs. She struggled, but couldn't free herself. Her feet banged on every step, jarring her all the way up her spine.

Surely, someone on the lower levels heard that. Surely, someone would come investigate. Surely, someone would do something.

She elbowed the man, then tried to hit his face with her fists. When he pulled her onto the upper floor, she levered herself up on his arm and kicked him on his shins. He didn't even flinch. He continued to drag her. One of the other men joined him, and they flung her into that room.

She slid along the floor on her skirt, and nearly slammed into the wall. The men peered down at her.

"What do we do with her?" asked the man who had flushed.

The man who had dragged her reached down, and pulled her lips back so that he could look at her teeth like she was a horse. She tried to bite him again.

"Feisty bit of business," one of the other men said.

"Who are you, really?" the man who dragged her asked.

"Philippa Darcy," she snapped, using the name she used in this period. "I'm expected in Mr. Morgan's office."

"It's eleven-thirty," one of the men said to the others.

The man who dragged her grinned. "Then I'll wager that Mr. Morgan won't mind if you don't show up. He probably won't even notice."

"He *will*," she said, keeping to the game. "He'll notice. He'll send someone searching for me."

"Nice try, honey," said the man who dragged her. "But you girls aren't that important to anyone in the House of Morgan. No one except your boss even knows your name."

"What do we do with her?" the man who flushed asked again.

"We can't send her home for another 31 minutes," said the man with the shoes.

Her heart rate increased. They knew. They knew about the bomb; they probably knew that she didn't belong here.

"What's really going on?" she asked.

"Ah, honey," said the man who dragged her. "That's above your pay grade. It's strictly need-to-know."

She struggled to her feet. Damn the skirt. Her legs caught in its folds.

"I think I need to know," she said, with more bravado than she felt.

"And you will know," the man who dragged her said. Then he grinned. "All in good time."

And all of the men laughed, as if he had told a particularly witty joke.

Washington, D.C.
March 23, 2057 (Supposedly)

LANE WAS DEEP in his research when his assistant peeked her head in the door. He nearly snapped at her, but thought the better of it. Her lips were in a thin line, her hair slightly out of place. She looked frazzled, and one reason he had hired her was because she was the most unflappable person he had ever met.

"The Attorney General just called a meeting downstairs," she said. "He says it's urgent."

"I thought nothing was urgent in the Time Division," Lane said.

"Apparently," she said, "this is."

Manhattan
September 16, 1920

AT 11:55 AM, Charles Gage took his seat at the back of Fred Eberlin's New Street restaurant. The place smelled of frying meat and spilled beer. The table was sticky, and even in the middle of the day, the electric lights were on. They weren't very powerful, and they barely cut the gloom.

The waiter who had greeted him didn't want him to sit so far back.

"Wouldn't you rather have a seat up front by the window, sir?" he asked as Gage strode toward the back of the restaurant. "You can watch all of New York go by without moving a muscle."

"Not today," Gage said. Today, if he sat by that plate glass window, or any plate glass window within six blocks of Wall Street, he ran the risk of serious injury, maybe even death.

Even sitting this far back was a risk. But he wanted to be inside the time-guard. Within the hour, the police would block off sections of Wall Street, and he wouldn't be able to get in unless his paperwork was perfect.

He didn't want to rely on perfect paperwork. He wanted to rely on outsmarting whatever it was that had set up the time bubble in the first place.

The waiter sighed loudly. "The specials are on the board up front, sir, but I suppose I can recite them for you."

"I'd rather have a sarsaparilla," Gage said. He'd acquired a taste for the damn things on another job, ten years ago his time, but only a year before this one. He had a hunch that whatever the Coca-Cola company used to make the drink was bad for him, but he didn't care. It was a taste he couldn't get anywhen else. If, of course, he had time to drink it.

He pulled out his pocket watch. He'd set it to New York time the moment he arrived. He couldn't get to Washington D.C. on September 16, so he'd had to settle for Philadelphia which, for some reason, wasn't time-guarded at all. He took a train to Manhattan, and arrived at Penn Station at nine a.m. Then he'd walked down the island, and stopped near the Equitable Life Insurance Building, which, at 38 stories, was currently the tallest building in the city, if not the world.

He'd loitered outside for as long as he could, watching the cutthroat operatives of the outdoor Curb Market trade the junk stocks and bonds that the regular markets sneered at. Part of him was fascinated to see history in action. The Curb Market's annex was nearly finished, and these traders would move inside within the year. But for the moment, they acted like street vendors, waving their tickets and shouting to be heard.

But he couldn't simply observe them. He needed to keep an eye on the street. He was watching for a touring car with a New Jersey license plate. He was also looking for some sort of old wooden wagon being pulled by an elderly horse. The horse would end up in pieces all over Wall Street, as would the wagon. The touring car would end up on its side.

Smart money believed that the car rear-ended the wagon, which had probably come from the DuPont Powder Works with a load of dynamite. Manhattan had banned the transport of explosives on its streets during the daylight hours, but that didn't mean that companies followed the rules.

He saw the touring car, recognizing its plate—NJ24246— and realized that the man who claimed to be the chauffer in the news reports looked nothing like the man driving. Then Gage saw a brand new wagon being pulled by an elderly horse. He wished he could take video, but he didn't dare. He was already attracting enough attention by standing outside the Equitable Building.

He'd slipped through the crowds and made his way to the restaurant where he sat now, wondering if the things he had seen had any meaning whatsoever.

Not that he was here for the bombing. He wasn't. He was here to find Philippa D'Arco, or Darcy as they called her. Her image was stamped—literally—inside his mind. One of those chips that the investigators for the Justice Department used on occasion. He knew what she looked like when she walked, talked, laughed, as if he had known her well. He wouldn't be able to miss her any more than a lover or her own family would have.

If Gage saw her. If he found her.

He wasn't entirely sure she was still here. He had telephoned the House of Morgan that morning, and asked if she was working. He'd been told that secretaries did not receive personal calls while at work, and then someone had asked his name.

"I'm her father," he had lied. "Her mother's gravely ill. I would like to speak to her."

"You may do so during her regular luncheon," the young man who had answered the phone told him. "All female secretaries take luncheon beginning at noon."

"But she is in the office?" Gage pressed.

"She signed in at 7:45 am, sir. Good day." And the young man had hung up.

So Gage had three pieces of information to take back with him. Philippa D'Arcy had shown up to work. The chauffer on the touring car did not look like his photograph in the papers from the hearings. And the wagon that might or might not have been carrying the dynamite was brand new.

The waiter set down a tall glass with the greenish brown liquid foaming inside. Gage picked it up, hoping for one sip before all hell broke loose—

And then the world went white. A sound, louder than anything he'd ever heard, shook the building. The air turned fire hot, then evaporated, and his lungs ached. He dove under the table. Too late. Already shards of glass had slid their way here.

Everything went deadly quiet. Nothing. Not a single sound. Almost as if all of New York held its breath at the same moment.

And then someone moaned.

The waiter was crouched against the back wall. The two customers who had been sitting near the window were sprawled on the floor. Another waiter leaned against the counter, still clutching a plate of food.

Gage stood, ran his hands over his suit, checking to see if

he was uninjured. He was. He knocked some glass shards out of his hair, picked up his hat, and shook it off as well.

The screams were beginning, as were the cries for help.

He took a deep breath, tasting smoke, blood, and something acrid, but at least there was oxygen again. He steeled his shoulders, and stepped into what he knew would be the hardest few minutes of his life.

He had to step over the injured, pass the dumbstruck, avoid the helpless, and head for the door. It had been blown open by the force of the explosion. A young man sprawled on the steps, bleeding from a gash in the head. His trembling right hand reached for a spiked rail that had ripped through the shoulder of his suit.

That had to be George Lacina, who worked at Equitable Life Assurance, the man whose comment to *The New York World* had set off all sorts of alarms in 2057. Lacina said that he later noticed that all the buttons on his coat had come off, and his watch was ten minutes slow.

Almost as if time had stopped. Or gone backward. Or rippled.

All signs of a time-guard.

Gage glanced at his pocket watch. It appeared to have stopped. But as he looked at it, the second hand moved. He needed to do the same.

It was easier said than done. Hundreds of people poured out of buildings, hurried down stairs, and ran away from the financial district. Some of them bleeding, many of them covered in glass or plaster, all of them looking terrified.

He had to go upstream, pushing through them all, careful not to fall or he would be trampled to death. All the while his feet slipped on blood or severed limbs or body parts he couldn't identify.

A woman on fire screamed as she ran past him. A man tackled her from the side, wrapping her in a coat.

Gage pretended he didn't see, reminded himself it was history. When that didn't work, he lied to himself that it was a virtual simulation—and he'd been through hundreds of those. Thousands. He couldn't help these people. They were more than a century dead, and for most, this was the worst day of their lives. But he couldn't reach out, couldn't do anything.

He had to find Philippa.

He reached the House of Morgan, pushed his way up the narrow steps toward the open doors. People still poured out, but he didn't see her among them. He caught some of the women who looked unhurt.

"Philippa," he said. "Where's Philippa?"

Mostly they shook their heads, then shook him off. One heavyset older woman frowned at him, said, "She went … necessary. But … an hour ago."

Only she was gone before he could parse out what that meant. Or what he hoped it had meant. Philippa had gone to the ladies room an hour before and had never come back.

If she was a smart little time traveler, she would have vanished by now, safe back in 2057, inside the Bubble, making her report. But he was here because she hadn't done that. Her body hadn't shown up, her chip hadn't activated, her failsafe device hadn't returned.

He knew his chip would survive a blast—he'd been through half a dozen of them, not to mention the fact that everything was tested for all kinds of conditions—so he doubted her equipment had failed.

He kept grabbing people, asking, "Philippa?" and getting no response.

Except from a red-haired young man, wearing shirt-sleeves, and ripped pants.

"Thought I saw her upstairs," he said, voice trembling. "Lordy, I hope she's all right."

Gage nodded, kept moving, found the stairs, tried to ignore what he saw. Couldn't ignore all of it. The young man held into place by something large—a bit of wall, maybe?—pinning his skull to his teller cage. The man with the broken leg trying to help another man bleeding from the face. The woman ripping pieces of her skirt and using them to tie off oozing wounds.

Above the trading floor, the glass dome that marked this part of the House of Morgan creaked. People screamed and dove for the walls. He didn't. He knew it wouldn't collapse.

Junius Morgan, carrying a wounded man toward the door. His face was scorched, his clothing blood-covered, but he seemed determined.

All of these people were heroes. Gage wasn't. He couldn't be. He had to keep searching for Philippa.

He explored several floors, saw more wounded, but no more dead, avoided some of the dazed victims, and kept searching. He didn't see her and no one seemed to know where she was.

He spent nearly two hours inside the House of Morgan, exploring each room, seeing all the damage—which was much more considerable than the papers ever made it out to be—and he found no trace of her.

It was as if she had followed instructions and vanished. Only she hadn't.

Finally, when he walked out of the bank, exhausted and covered in dirt and blood, he braced himself. Time to assume his identity as a Pinkerton, pretending he'd been hired by the Equitable Company, since the House of Morgan was unofficially using William J. Burns's International Detective Agency.

He would find Philippa, or the parts of her, or what became of her, if he had to stay here for the next year to do so.

Washington, D.C.
March 23, 2057 (Supposedly)

THE CONFERENCE ROOM, bunkered under the building, was an unassuming little space, modeled on the White House's Situation Room. Bunkered, time-guarded with all the latest gadgetry, but so shielded that no one could travel in even from inside the Bubble itself.

Lane hated the little room. It looked like something out of time itself. Rectangular, with blond wood paneling, matching table, and the most uncomfortable blue chairs in the world, the room was always stuffy and tension-filled.

He was the last person to arrive, and as he pulled the door open, he had only seconds to prepare. No one had warned him that he faced not only the Attorney General, but Cabinet Secretaries from Treasury and Time as well. And, off in a corner, as if he were monitoring the meeting instead of participating in it, Brandon Carnelius, the Chairman of the Federal Reserve.

Lane had barely gotten the door closed when the Attorney General said, "You need to recall Charles Gage from 1920."

Kayla Huntingdon was not known for her diplomatic skills, something that had gotten her into trouble with Congress more than once. Sometimes Lane wondered how she ever made it through her confirmation.

"We lost an operative," Lane said. "And we've found some anomalies."

"We know," said Noah Singh. He ran Treasury. He *was* known for his diplomacy, not that it showed at the moment. "Recall him anyway."

Lane knew better than to remind Singh that he did not work for Treasury. Annabelle Tsu, the Time Secretary, nodded. "We have decided. We're going to leave the time-guard in place."

"We didn't create it," Lane said. "I've researched. It didn't come from the government."

"Not technically," Singh said. "But you needn't worry about it."

Lane looked at Huntingdon. He realized from the set of her full mouth that she was furious. She had not been informed about something. Tsu's long red fingernails tapped on the tabletop. Apparently she hadn't been informed either.

"You want to tell me what's going on?" Lane asked. He'd directed the question at his boss, Huntingdon, but he didn't care who answered.

"Technically, you don't have the security clearance," Singh

said. "We've decided to bring you into this, since you might run into an anomaly, as you call it, again, and we need you to be prepared."

Huntingdon looked down, her blond hair covering her face. Lane had seen her do that before. It was a deliberate move so that no one could see her expression. Yep, she was pissed. And he had a hunch he was about to be.

"I'm not sure that you're aware of the fact that the Federal Reserve System was founded in 1913," Singh said.

"I know my history," Lane said.

"Let him speak," Tsu said quietly.

"And worked with other central bankers in other nations during the various wars. The Fed's powers expanded after the Great Depression, the Great Recession, and of course, the recent Currency Crisis," Singh said. He sounded like every bad professor Lane had ever had.

"Let me cut through the bullshit for you," Huntingdon said. "Somewhere along the way, these so-called financial geniuses figured the only way to control monetary policy was to change it. By going backwards."

"What?" Lane blinked. No one was supposed to alter major historical events just because they hadn't worked properly. Or what this generation thought of as properly. "They can't do that. It's not legal."

"We started our policy before it was illegal," Carnelius intoned from his corner. As if that made it right. There were laws in place to cover such things. Otherwise someone could go back in time and do something that wasn't a crime then, but was now, and be completely immune from prosecution.

Lane started to say that, but Tsu shook her head. Tsu, who looked as angry as Huntingdon.

"Forgive me, sir," Lane said to the Fed Chair, knowing he was out of turn. "But we're all forbidden from messing with Time."

"Yes, we are" Singh said, taking the focus off Carnelius. "The Fed knows that now. But they started before the rest of us. Interestingly enough, they had time travel devices long before anyone else did. And they did things that they've been trying to clean up ever since. You're probably most familiar with the Flash Crash of 2010? That was an error on the part of the time travelers from the International Monetary Fund, who are tied into this as well."

"I don't understand," Lane said.

"Someone," Huntingdon said, "and no one will say *who*..." and with that she looked at Carnelius, "tried to use a time device in 1920. And then tried to cover it up. Which is why all the original detectives from the Bureau of Investigation to the New York Police Department to the private detectives had no real idea what happened, because *all* of their theories were true."

Lane got cold. A messy cover-up led to conflicting time stories, which led to bad investigations, which lead to chaos that often cost lives. Like it had in this instance.

"We cannot investigate the so-called bombing without making matters worse," Huntingdon said. "So call off your people. And when you hit a similar time-guarded moment related to something financial, check before you send investigators into the past."

"Wouldn't it be easier if we knew what periods to avoid?" Lane asked Huntingdon.

Her lower jaw moved slightly before she responded. "It would. And yet, apparently, the Fed is not in the business of making our lives easier."

Carnelius shook his head slightly, as if no one understood him.

Lane filtered several responses before he said the one thing he felt he had the right to say, "We've been working on the Wall Street Bombing for nearly a year of our time. We've used a lot of resources. Why has this just come up now?"

"Because," Carnelius said, "one of your operatives stumbled on some of ours."

"Who?" Lane asked. "And when?"

"In 1920. Miss Philippa—Darcy? D'Arco? She stumbled on my people. The moment they found out who she was, they sent word to us."

Time didn't work that way, but the language didn't keep up. They'd found out in 1920, but when had they discovered it in 2057? Or had they? How had word gotten back? Lane didn't know, and he had a hunch everyone would say he didn't have the right to ask.

"When can we get her back?" he asked. That at least, would be a victory. He wouldn't have lost an investigator to this ridiculous operation.

"They won't give her back," Huntingdon said, the frustration clear in her voice.

"See here, Kayla. It's not quite like that," Singh said.

"She can't come back," Tsu said. "She knows too much."

"She's ours now," Carnelius said. "You don't need to worry about her. We'll take good care of her."

"Like you took good care of Wall Street in 1920?" Lane snapped.

"Prescott," Singh said. "Some respect."

"Yes, respect would've been nice, wouldn't it?" Lane said as he got up. "Thirty-eight dead, hundreds more injured, in what history considers the worst act of terrorism on American soil until a bombing in Oklahoma City in 1995? All caused by some idiots mishandling time travel for the Federal Reserve."

"Technically, it wasn't us," Carnelius said. "We're not the only Central Bank with time travel capabilities."

"Oh, that makes it so much better." Lane spread his hands on the tabletop and looked at Huntingdon. "I'm going to tender my resignation."

"And I'll have to refuse it," she said. "With this kind of secret, you have just become a lifer in the Time Division."

Lane's breath caught. He felt a moment of terror that he

then suppressed. "You can't do that. I serve at the whim of the President."

"And at whose whim does the President serve?" Tsu muttered.

"Enough," Singh said. "This meeting is over. And it never happened."

"Of course not." Lane felt dizzy. "Just like I never lost an investigator."

"You didn't lose her," Carnelius said. "You simply transferred her to a better paying job."

"I did nothing of the sort," Lane said. "I want that on the record."

"What record?" Huntingdon asked. "This meeting never happened."

Lane tilted his head back. His brain hurt. And this wasn't even a time paradox. It was a political one, with real repercussions on real people's lives.

"When will you return her to us?" he asked.

"We won't," Carnelius said. "She's ours now. Forever."

That would have sounded ominous outside of the Bubble. Inside it, it was damn near terrifying.

"I suppose you won't tell me what that means," Lane said.

"It means she's elsewhen." Carnelius stood. "And that's all I'm going to say."

Manhattan
September 1, 2088 (Supposedly)

"YOU'VE GOT TO BE KIDDING," Philippa said. She sat on what looked like air, a clear chair that was more comfortable than anything she felt in weeks. "I have to stay here?"

"Not here, exactly," said the man who had dragged her. His name was Roland Karinki, and he worked for the Time Unit in the Federal Reserve. At the moment, they were in the Manhattan Fed, in a room that literally vanished in the clouds. "You're free to leave this job, to do whatever you want."

"But I can't go home," she said.

"If by that you mean 2057, no, you cannot. It's forbidden to you now. But we can use your services here or in the distant past. We have a lot to do."

She tried not to look panicked. She tried not to *be* panicked. Her training had warned her that she might get stuck out of her time. It wasn't supposed to bother her. She was positively bloodless, after all.

But she didn't feel bloodless.

"I liked 2057," she said. "No, I loved 2057."

"I believe you," Karinki said. "At least you're not trying to lie to me by saying that you're leaving behind friends and family. I know Time Division forbids both of those."

"Not friends," she said, although if she were being truthful, she had not been encouraged to have good friends.

Which made her wonder about all those girls she'd worked with in the House of Morgan. Had they made it out safely? Were they badly wounded? Would she ever know?

"You'll like it better here," Karinki said. "I promise."

"Promises from a man who grabbed me and tossed me

into a room, then took me out of my life. Great. How do I know I can trust you?"

"Because," he said. "I have orders from your boss. Do you recall Prescott Lane? He left a file for you, which you can view at your leisure."

She narrowed her gaze. "I know nothing about 2088. You could have faked it."

"I could have," Karinki said. "But I didn't. *We* didn't. And we will help you adjust."

She leaned her head back, and thought for a moment. She was somewhen else. That was what she wanted when she woke up this morning in that wretched two-room flat, with two smelly girls beside her on a flea-ridden mattress. And she had a hunch the food would be better than it had been in 1920. The attitudes would be better as well. And then there was the matter of comfort.

Maybe she was positively bloodless. Because she could feel herself transitioning to the new when.

"I need a hot shower," she said. "Some new clothes. And a bed in a place that has climate control."

"That's easy," Karinki said. "How about dinner?"

"Sure," she said. "Alone. In my new apartment. With all kinds of information at my fingertips about the last thirty-one years. I won't make a decision until I know what my options are."

"Fair enough," he said, and then extended his hand. "Welcome to the future."

She looked at his palm. It was clean, but it had bite marks on the fleshy part that he hadn't yet cleaned up.

"It sure as hell better be nicer than the past," she said.

"Time periods are never one thing," he said. "You should know that."

She did know it. Maybe better than he did.

Maybe better than anyone.

She looked out that window at Lower Manhattan. Sunlight reflected off the Equitable Building struggling to survive between skyscrapers she couldn't identify. Through the buildings' canyons, she saw the Upper Bay, Battery Park, and a clean Statue of Liberty. Saw New Jersey in the distance.

"What month is it?" she asked.

He grinned. "September."

She looked outside again, but not down this time. Up, like people on the sidewalks in 1920. She saw a clear blue September sky. The kind that promised one of those spectacular New York days, the kind that made you wonder why you lived anywhere else.

"I'm staying in Manhattan," she said. "I don't care when. But I do care where."

He studied her for a moment, then nodded. "We can arrange that."

"Good," she said. "Because I wouldn't work for you any other way."

Pulphouse
FICTION MAGAZINE

THE NEWEST COLLECTIONS

pulphousemagazine.com

MINIONS
AT WORK
I know we're a hundred miles from the nearest ROAD, but I have the most UNCANNY feeling we're being FOLLOWED!
TOTAL SUPER HEROES NOPE
IRREGULAR MAINTENANCE
BY J. STEVEN YORK

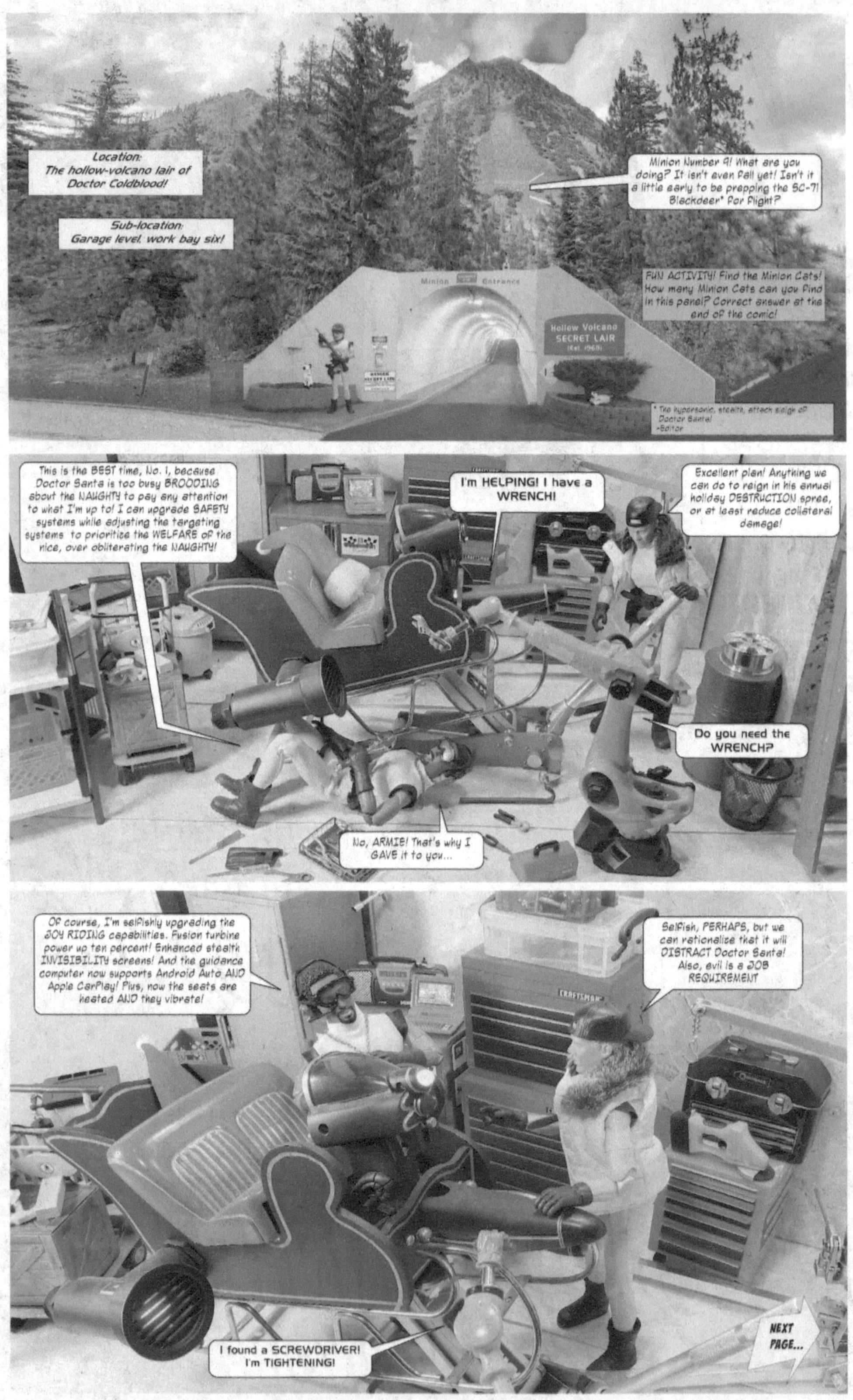

Location:
The hollow-volcano lair of
Doctor Coldblood!

Sub-location:
Garage level: work bay six!

Minion Entrance

Hollow Volcano
SECRET LAIR
(Est. 1969)

Minion Number 9! What are you doing? It isn't even Fall yet! Isn't it a little early to be prepping the SC-7! Blackdeer* for flight?

FUN ACTIVITY! Find the Minion Cats! How many Minion Cats can you find in this panel? Correct answer at the end of the comic!

* The hypersonic, stealth, attack sleigh of Doctor Santa!
~Editor

This is the BEST time, No. 1, because Doctor Santa is too busy BROODING about the NAUGHTY to pay any attention to what I'm up to! I can upgrade SAFETY systems while adjusting the targeting systems to prioritize the WELFARE of the nice, over obliterating the NAUGHTY!

I'm HELPING! I have a WRENCH!

Excellent plan! Anything we can do to reign in his annual holiday DESTRUCTION spree, or at least reduce collateral damage!

Do you need the WRENCH?

No, ARMIE! That's why I GAVE it to you...

Of course, I'm selfishly upgrading the JOY RIDING capabilities! Fusion turbine power up ten percent! Enhanced stealth INVISIBILITY screens! And the guidance computer now supports Android Auto AND Apple CarPlay! Plus, now the seats are heated AND they vibrate!

Selfish, PERHAPS, but we can rationalize that it will DISTRACT Doctor Santa! Also, evil is a JOB REQUIREMENT

I found a SCREWDRIVER! I'm TIGHTENING!

NEXT PAGE...

Answer to "FUN ACTIVITY!"

Due to a "lab accident," Minion Cat has become QUANTUM INDETERMINATE, and therefore (in this timeline, anyway) the answer is always both, and neither, ONE or ZERO!
The illusion that there are MULTIPLE Minion Cats is the result of time and space SHUTTERING taking place BETWEEN the intervals of PLANCK time, making Minion Cat the FASTEST thing in the universe! Assuming he (or she, or they) exist at all, of course!
Did you maybe think the answer was something like -- FOUR? Geeze! Do we have explain EVERYTHING to you numskulls?
Well, the good news is, you might have MINION potential...

www.ingramcontent.com/pod-product-compliance
Lightning Source LLC
Chambersburg PA
CBHW010732100726

47899CB00009B/3010